The Ghosts
Of
Hanson House

A Haunting In Kingston Novella

MICHELLE DOREY

ISBN: 978-1-927984
ISBN-13: 978-1-927984-92-5

DEDICATION

To my granddaughters Emma and Julia

CONTENTS

MICHELLE DOREY

ACKNOWLEDGMENTS

To my hometown Kingston, Ontario and all who live here.

PROLOGUE: 1912 & 1929

April, 1912

The frigid North Atlantic water was like glass in the dark night. The only movements on its surface were the ripples caused by the oars from the lifeboats. The final heave of the stern of the ship slipping below the surface had taken place twenty minutes earlier, and those still trapped in the water were succumbing one after another to the frozen embrace of the ocean.

Soon, all was still. The dead floated in their now useless lifebelts and those fortunate enough to have secured a spot on one of the boats sat aboard in stunned silence. It had all happened so quickly. From the first shudders and groans of the iceberg striking their ship to now was barely two hours.

The only light was from the cold stars above as there was no moon. Starlight dappled across the small ripples of water, across still bodies, and the flotsam of a disaster that claimed over a thousand souls.

A child's doll drifted lazily away from a small, almost frozen hand. Its owner had been in steerage, and by the time she and her family had managed to navigate through the maze of the lower corridors and scramble up onto the main deck, all of the lifeboats had already cast off.

Her mother had found her a discarded lifebelt; one tossed aside by an older gentleman who had already accepted his own fate. She strapped it onto her daughter, her only child, with shivering hands.

Loud roars from the bursting seams of the boilers in the engine room created a cacophony across the listing deck, followed by an enormous lurch as the stern of the ship was lifted.

Her eyes wide with panic and horror, the mother lifted her daughter. She was but six years old and small for her age.

"God bless you and keep you, Katie!" She covered the child's still face with kisses. Pointing to one of the boats still near the hull, she said, "Now swim as hard as you can for that boat!"

With all her might she flung the child over the railing and into the sea.

It may have been a mercy on the poor woman that as soon as she released her daughter another, more powerful lurch knocked her from her feet. She didn't see her daughter land face first in the water from a height of over forty feet, and not move.

Even so, her unconscious hand still clutched dolly. For a while.

There was no witness to the dolly coming free and floating away.

No witness saw the red glow spark behind the dolly's glass eye that night to remember.

The entity within it reveled in the panic and horror all around it. It gorged on the sorrow and pain of this night; a glutton at a feast. It meandered through the lifeboats, feeling the horror and terror of the survivors emanating and sating its eternal hunger.

As it drew away from the scene, once again the entity fell into a slumber. It had oozed across the world for millennia; there would always be another feast.

***

In March of 1929 Desmond Hanson waded onto the shore of Wolfe Island. He turned and gave a short wave to Connor Finn who was already reversing the small motor on his dory. "It'll be two weeks, Connor?" he called.

"Of course! Good work tonight, and I'll be letting you know lad!"

Lad. Connor was but six months older. But the fifty dollars he put in Desmond's pocket for the night's work gave him the seniority. Desmond patted his pocket. The farm was doing fairly well, but the extra money every few weeks for loading and unloading crates of whiskey across the bay into the U.S. made hard living easier. Unlike the other farmers on the island, he wasn't worried about getting enough money together for the Spring planting. What was in his pocket would keep him from having to sign any promissory note at the bank this year. God bless Connor, even if he got on a high horse every now and then.

He walked along the shoreline towards his home. He always came ashore a half mile away, just in case the coppers had been trailing them. A roundabout way home also gave him a chance to shake off the nerves. Rum running was as dangerous as it was profitable, especially at the delivery. In other areas, it was known that business rivals Stateside thought nothing of hijacking the competition's goods. And leaving bodies behind.

But that was that. He had plenty of time now to relax before he'd have to get all willy-nilly again. And if a case of the whim whams every few weeks was what it took to keep from bowing and scraping before a banker, well that was fine with him.

He glanced up at the sky. Connor always preferred making his deliveries on a moonless night. If there were cops out there, why make their job easier? But Lord a'mighty, the stars were beautiful; not a cloud!

His foot stumbled on a jutting rock on the shore and he caught himself before falling. He'd better take care and watch his step. This section of the island wasn't known for its smooth beaches after all.

"What the?" he said out loud, stopping in his tracks.

Resting on the shore was the most beautiful doll he had ever seen; lovelier than any that were in the pages of the Eaton's Christmas Catalogue! It was in a sitting position, the waters of the St. Lawrence river almost lapping at its feet. He bent over and picked it up.

He examined it. It was a stuffed china dolly, its head, hands and feet made of porcelain, and its body some sort of leatherette. This had to be from Europe; France most likely. He tilted its head and the beautiful blue glass eyes closed. Lifting it, they opened.

His hand brushed over the blue satin dress, with a pinafore over it. He turned it over in his hands. Not a mark nor stain on it.

He gazed across the river. Some rich child on a boat must have dropped it overboard by accident. And that must have been some time ago, as the doll was completely dry.

He held the toy up in front of him. "Irene is going to love you to death, dearie!" he said out loud. "What do you think of that?" He tilted the doll and its eyes closed demurely. "And she'll love me even more for bringing you home to her!" he added with a chuckle.

As if it were a newborn, he put it over his shoulder. Picking up his pace, he headed home.

He didn't see how the dolly's eyes glowed red for a moment and dimmed again.

Another feast...

4

CHAPTER ONE

September 1956

Danny cowered next to his bike as he leaned it against the front yard fence. Despite the autumn chill, his fingers were sweaty on the handle bars. The Hanson farm house loomed at the end of the tangled mess of weeds lining the dirt driveway, while the dark windows above the front porch were like eyes glaring straight through him.

"You're scared, aren't you? I told you that you'd chicken out when we got here." Allen's ferret eyes stared at the dilapidated house. "I'm not scared! I'm goin' in." He leaned his bike against the rusty wire fence and shoved the gate open, totally ignoring the 'No Trespassing' sign.

For a moment, Danny froze, watching Allen. His heart pounded faster and he forced himself to take a deep, slow breath. If he didn't go through with this, Allen would blab it all over school. He could hear him now, 'Danny Baker was too scared to even cross the fence. A real chicken shit.' The gang of boys in school would hang on every word and sneer at Danny. But the worst would be Abby Wilkes. She was bound to hear and she sure wouldn't think too highly of him then. Just when she was starting to warm up to him, even letting him walk her home after school the week before. When they started high school next year, he didn't want to be known as chicken.

He let his bike fall to the ground and even though his legs were limp noodles he sprinted to catch up with Allen. "I'm not scared. Wait up, will ya?"

Allen turned and looked past him, back to the dirt road they'd just rode down. "It's 'Injun Joe'. He followed us." He rolled his eyes and let out a loud groan.

Danny turned and sure enough, with legs pumping hard and ebony hair blowing back from his high forehead, Frank Grant rode fast to catch up. Danny smiled and felt the knot in his stomach loosen a bit. He turned to Allen and spat the words at him. "That's a shitty thing to say! His name's Frank."

"Yeah? Like I care." Allen nudged Danny with his shoulder. "C'mon. Let's do this if you're not too chicken."

Danny huffed a long sigh. Frank was a great guy if anyone ever took the time to get past the fact he was native. Certainly Allen and the other guys never bothered. He turned to shadow Allen, trudging slowly across the yard to the front step. It sagged lower on one side and the wood was a beaten down gray. Only faint traces of the white it had once worn peeked through. When Allen stepped onto the first step, the creak of the board sent a shiver scuttling down Danny's spine.

A crow cawed and then beat the air with its wings, escaping the stand of spindly elm trees next to the house. Danny jerked at the sound before turning his gaze to the weather-beaten wooden door hanging slightly ajar. Allen was on the top step, edging closer, his footsteps creeping forward with barely a whisper of sound.

With one foot on the bottom step and one still on the ground, Danny held his breath, watching his friend push the door wide.

Allen stood, gaping at the darkness inside for a few moments. He turned and his narrow eyes dared Danny. "Well? What are you waiting for?"

"Hey! Don't go in there, you guys!"

Danny's head jerked around at Frank's voice.

Frank was still on the other side of the gate, his long dungaree clad legs straddling his bike while his jacket hung loose and open. "Come back, Danny! That place is dangerous! It's haunted!"

"Shove off, Frank!" Allen's voice was like the crack of a whip right beside Danny's head. He sneered down at Danny, speaking softer now. "He's a chicken-shit, redskin. We'll show him we're not afraid." He turned and took a step to the doorway, peering inside.

Danny regarded Frank like he was a life line. But he could no more grab hold to any hope of getting out of this. How had he let Allen talk him into riding to the Hanson farm? There was no use trying to reason with him; when he got something in his head, he never let it go.

His legs were rubbery as he walked up the steps. The air that drifted from the house was clammy and smelled like decay. Horizontal strips of wood showed through parts of the wall where the plaster had fallen off—like the rotten bones of a skeleton.

When his eyes adjusted to the dim interior, he could make out a faded leaf pattern on the threadbare rug runner, bordered on each side with an oily, black wooden floor. Wallpaper hung in shreds, along with sheets of spider webs on the walls beside him. He pulled his arms in closer to his body, recoiling at the walls around him.

Allen took a few steps to an archway on the right and peered inside. Pointing a finger, his voice was barely above a whisper when he spoke. "Do ya suppose it happened in there?"

Danny gut was a twisted knot. Yeah. That was the story. It was the living room or historically called the parlour, and that's where they said Mrs. Hanson killed herself. He turned to look at the set of stairs leading to the second floor—to the bedrooms where the kids and husband had lain, their lives choked out from the poisoned meal she'd served them. He shivered and tugged the collar of his jacket higher on his neck.

At the sound of Allen's footsteps he turned in time to see

him slip through the arch and disappear into another room through the parlor. He slowly followed him, like he was walking through a mine field as his gaze darted over the furniture left there. A tattered green sofa with gray tufts of stuffing teased from the seat and one arm, looked to be home to mice and other disgusting creatures. Attached to the dark window frame with a gossamer of webs, a wooden rocking chair hunched motionless on the wooden floor. Curtains hung in dusty folds from a rust covered rod above the window.

His face was tight peering around the room. He wasn't sure what exactly he'd expected but seeing furniture still there was definitely not it. It made the stories he'd heard seem more real somehow. Here was the furniture they'd sat on, reading a book or talking about the events of the day—at least until that awful, fateful night when the mother had gone crazy and murdered them all. What kind of madness would drive a mother to kill her own children?

Allen slipped by him, walking quickly out of the room. His eyebrows bobbed and there was a grin on his face. "Creepy, huh?"

Danny's eyes narrowed. Entering the house on a dare was one thing but to actually enjoy this was sacrilegious.

He continued following his friend down the hall into a room that ran the width of the house. There were two windows bordering a back door and along one wall was a set of cabinets and a counter. He stopped short when his gaze lowered to take in the old wood fired cook stove and a beat up table dominating the space. The sight of dishes covered with half eaten food set out on the table, along with cutlery made his blood run cold. There were even pots still sitting on the stove. Why would there still be food out like this after all these years?

Oh my God. Was it the remnants of that poisoned meal? The wife hadn't even cleaned up before she took her own life. But why hadn't she eaten the meal like the rest of them? Maybe the death that she'd chosen—hanging, breaking her bloody neck—had been easier than what the rest of them went through.

Danny's stomach roiled as he choked down the bile in the back of his mouth. "Allen? I've seen enough."

Allen snorted. "I knew it—knew you'd chicken out." He smiled. "Not me, though. I'm gonna see it all—see where they died." He spun on his heels and his footsteps were bolder now, going down the hall and then thudding quickly up the stairs.

Danny took a few deep breaths and closed his eyes, blocking the sight of the food and dishes. He HAD to do this. And now there was Frank outside, another witness who would tell that he chickened out. He trudged after Allen, going cautiously up the stairs, to the rooms where the kids had died. From the stories he heard they weren't even ten years old. Just little kids, way younger than him.

He wasn't even halfway up the stairs when Allen's voice cried out, "Holy cow! Hurry! Have a look at this, will ya?"

Darting to the top of the stairs, he followed the sound until he came upon Allen in a room down the hall. Allen's mouth was gaped open looking at a narrow bed, where stained bedclothes lay strewn. From the dark reddish brown, the stains had to be blood. Was that the way the poison worked? You threw up blood? Danny stepped back into the doorway, the gorge in his mouth rising again.

THUD!

His head jerked around and his heart leapt up into his throat! "What was that?" The loud noise had come from the floor below.

Allen jerked his head towards the door, his blue eyes seeming to pop out on his cheeks. He panted and then a nervous smile twitched his lips. "It's that stupid Injun, trying to scare us." He strode by Danny and stood at the top of the staircase. "Buzz off, Frank! Nice try but it didn't—"

Allen jerked forward, as if someone behind him had given him a hard shove. He stumbled down the first few steps as Danny dove to grab at him and missed. With horror, Danny watched Allen somersault down. He let out a single shriek before slamming into the floor at the bottom of the stairs...

and then was still.

"No!" Danny raced down the stairs and knelt next to his friend. Allen's eyes were open but his head was almost turned completely around facing backwards. The trickle of blood flowing out his nostril was the only movement in the boy's face. Oh my God! It couldn't be.

Allen was DEAD!

Footsteps thudded hard on the floor above him. Danny's head spun to look back up the stairs. Someone was up there. And they were coming his way.

He jumped up and raced across the hall to the front door. The door knob turned but it wouldn't open. The footsteps were now on the stairs! He yanked on the door, pulling with all his might but it wouldn't budge.

He pounded the door with his fists. "HELP! Help me, Frank!" It was coming and he had to get out of there, fast!

At the thud behind him, he spun to see. There was a swirling black mass, like smoke hovering just above Allen's body. His heart raced so fast, he couldn't breathe! What the hell was that thing? The air around him became cold...so cold he could see his breath clouding in front of his face. It passed over Allen's still figure and was oozing down the hall towards him. Oh my God, it was going to get him!

Abandoning the front door, he raced down the hall to the kitchen back door. Once more he yanked at it but it remained shut solid. All the while, the thuds of footsteps sounded from the hallway! If that thing...whatever the hell it was, touched him, he'd be a goner. He didn't know how he knew that, but he just knew it was true!

Danny raced back into the parlour and grabbed the rocking chair next to the window. He hurled it at the glass. The chair shattered, with one of the curved bottom flying off and landing with a bang on the floor. It had bounced OFF the glass when it should have gone through it! Oh shit! What the hell was happening?

"Danny? Are you all right?" Frank, on the outside of the front door, pounded his fists on it. "Why won't this *open*!"

Danny could hardly breathe when he raced out of the room. The black cloud began to fade and move back over Allen and then slowly go up the stairs. He crouched and slowly crept back up the hallway, watching the stairs in case that THING came back. He touched the doorknob and pulled his hand back quickly. It was cold as ice. Above him, there was a soft murmur, like people whispering.

From the top of the stairs he heard the footsteps again. But now there was a LOT of them. The black mass again turned onto the landing. It was bigger this time, filling the stairwell as it oozed downward once more.

Terror froze him as he watched its relentless progress.

At the crash of breaking glass, he startled, then raced through the archway to the parlour. A rusty metal milk can lay amid a heap of glass and splintered wood. Frank's eyes were rimmed with white gaping in at him through the hole he'd created.

"What's happening in there? The door's stuck and you're screaming! What's going on? Where's Allen?" Frank was looking past Danny's shoulder.

Danny's feet crunched the shards of glass and then he gripped the sides of the window frame cutting his hands on the shards still left in the frame. "Danny, where's Allen?" His jet black eyes bored into Danny's. He clutched Danny's arms and yanked him through the opening, tumbling him to the ground. Leaning in, he yelled. "Allen! Come on!"

Danny got to his feet, wiping his bloody hands on his pants. "He was thrown down the stairs! He's dead!"

"He what? Who threw him, Danny? You?" Frank's eyes widened in fear.

"No! Not me!" Danny pointed through the window opening. "THAT!"

Frank turned to see the black roiling mass begin to ooze into the parlour and froze in place. "Ubba, nuggha..."

Danny yanked on his arm. "Frank! We've got to get out of here! Hurry before it gets us!"

Like a pair of commandos in a war movie they threw

themselves over the porch railing, landing on their feet. But Frank's foot landed on a heavy rock, twisting and snapping his ankle with a loud crack. He shrieked in pain.

Danny saw Frank sprawled on the ground, his foot twisted to the side.

"I broke it!" Frank gripped his ankle with both hands, his face screwed up tight.

"C'mon Frank! We gotta go!" Danny stepped back and tugged on Frank's arm to help him up.

"No! You go!" Tears filled Frank's eyes and he rocked back and forth still holding his ankle. "I can't." He was scrabbling on his butt as best he could away from the house.

"I'm not leaving without you! C'mon!" Danny tightened his grip on Frank's arm, and pulled, lifting him upright. Frank was bigger than him and he grunted with the strain, but he finally managed to pull him upright. "C'mon! Like a three legged race!"

Together the two boys managed to hobble across the yard. They were almost at the gate. Not much farther.

Behind them, an earth shattering scream broke the stillness, sending new waves of fear through their very bones. They staggered and slipped though the opening of the gate and Danny picked up his bike. Frank managed to ride on the seat while Danny stood, his legs working like an Olympic sprinter on the pedals. Clouds of dust rose after them as he pedaled the bike down the dirt road away from Hanson farm.

CHAPTER TWO

The Present

Emma set her suitcase on the lower bunk and flipped the lid open. Inside were all the clothes and make-up she would need for her month's stay on the farm. She turned to her younger sister, watching her cram clothes into the bottom two drawers of the antique dresser.

"Don't shove your dress in there. Hang it up. You know you've got to have something nice for church." Emma shook her head and began sorting through her own case, lifting a stack of folded T shirts in her hands. She walked over to the dresser and tugged the top drawer open to set them inside. The antique wood whispered softly when she closed it and a waft of camphor drifted into her nose.

Julia stood up, her big blue eyes meeting Emma's scowl in the mirror topping the dresser. "I don't see why we have to go to church. Mom and Dad never do, except at Christmas." Her shoulders slumped and she sighed.

Emma nudged her younger sister with her hand and her voice dropped to a whisper. "Shh! Nana and Grandpa will hear you!"

Julia pouted. "I don't care—"

Emma sighed. "Don't be such a brat, Julia. You're 10, not five."

Julia crossed her arms and stared at her big sister defiantly. "Oh what a big shot! Just because you start high school next year doesn't make you the boss of everything," she hissed.

"C'mon, Julia! It's Nana and Grandpa I'm talking about!" She kept her voice low. "Just because we aren't religious doesn't mean it's not important to them. You've got to show some respect, Julia."

Julia's chin rose high and her eyes flashed when she spun to face Emma. "I don't care! What does it matter? Think they'll send us packing? We can only hope!"

Emma could only stare silently at her sister. It was true that neither one of them had wanted to come to the farm. A month during the summer was a long time when they both could have been enjoying their friends at home, and involved with the sports they loved.

But Nana and Grandpa had been so happy when they arrived. She looked down at the floor. "Just be quiet about that stuff, okay? Remember, it's their last summer on the island. We won't ever have to do this again."

At the chirp of her cell phone, Emma reached in her backpack. It was her best friend, Ginny, sending a text.

I miss you already! Kyle is having a pool party for his birthday next weekend. Everyone is going, even Melissa! I'll keep an eye on her for you in case she flirts with him—the skank!

Emma's stomach sunk even lower and she flopped down on the bed. The thought of Kyle and Melissa together was too much. She'd had a crush on Kyle since like forever and now that she was out of town—especially at his birthday!—Melissa would hit on him. Well as much as a fourteen year old could be accused of hitting on anyone. This was going to be a long month.

"Emma! Julia! Come down! I see your Aunt's car pulling into the driveway! Your cousins are here!" Nana's voice drifted up the stairwell and through the open door of the big bedroom.

She couldn't help the long huffed sigh and roll of her eyes. Great. She hadn't seen Grace or Lily since the summer before and that was still too often. They...well actually Grace was always lording it over them that she lived in New York City! She'd heard *that* too many times.

Julia pranced across the floor, with an exaggerated sway of her hips and fluffing her curls with a limp hand, she batted her eyes and turned to face Emma. "I had *breakfast* at *Tiffany's* today and then went shopping at *Bloomies*!" She sniffed and turned her small nose high in the air. "Where on *earth* did you get that top you're wearing—Wal-Mart? Target? Hmph! Some deep discount place no doubt!" She clucked her tongue and then burst out laughing.

Emma giggled and then a full blown laugh burst from her chest. "You know, it's scary how well you do that! Don't let Grace catch you! She'd have a hissy fit!" She rose and then nodded to the open door. "C'mon. We'd better get this over with." Pausing for a moment, she gazed into her kid sister's eyes. "It's funny, isn't it? Aunt Cynthia is so nice. How did she ever have a snotty kid like Grace?"

Julia nodded and her smile fell. "Poor Lily doesn't stand a chance. Ever. No wonder she's so shy. She wouldn't say boo even if she was drowning."

"Yeah. If it was just Lily this month, I think I could stand it. But Grace..." Emma's lips pursed like she just sucked on a lemon and she left the room. Her feet clumped slowly down the wooden stairs and she walked down the short hallway to the kitchen, Julia on her tail.

Aunt Cynthia, with a wide smile on her lips, and her blue eyes crinkling in the outer corners, rushed forward and folded her arms over Emma, drawing her into a warm hug. "Emma! My, how you've grown! You're a regular little lady now." She held Emma at arm's length and her eyes wandered from her toes to her dark hair pulled back in a high pony tail. "Good Lord, you look sixteen! I can't believe you're only turning fourteen! Your father will have his hands full if you get any prettier!"

She turned her attention to Julia and it was then that Emma spied Grace just coming through the doorway. Just the top of a perfectly plucked eyebrow arched above the dark sunglasses. Her auburn hair was combed back, exposing a high porcelain forehead and a faint flush under highlighted cheekbones. She managed a small smile before sliding her glasses down her thin nose. "Hi Emma. It looks like we're spending some time together this summer, huh?"

"Hi Grace. Yeah. We're even sharing a bedroom, all of us. It'll be pretty cozy, all right." Emma could feel her stomach grow tight at the prospect of a month with her stuck up cousin. Not even a break at night to call home and whine at her parents for insisting she and Julia endure this. Spending time with her grandparents would be great, but Grace?

Nana had her arm around Lily and she stepped forward with the slight girl tucked into her. "Hasn't Lily grown, Emma? She's almost as tall as you are and she's only 11!"

Lily flashed a shy smile at Emma and then looked down at her feet. Her strawberry blonde hair hung loose around her thin face and she slouched forward, the neck of the yellow blouse askew revealing sharp collar bones. She looked like she'd like to fade into the background rather than be thrust forward to greet her cousins. If Grace was the hothouse flower, Lily was the shrinking violet.

Emma smiled and her hand rose to tuck some stray locks from Lily's cheek. "Hi Lily!" She glanced up into her Nana's sky-blue eyes and then back to Lily. "Yeah. It's hard to believe you're only a year older than Julia." Seeing Lily's face flush pink, she added, "Too bad for you *and* her. Age has its privilege. You guys get stuck on the top bunks."

Nana shook her head and snorted. "I could have set you up in separate rooms but..." She smiled. "This way, you'll get to know each other better. I remember as a young girl, sleep-over's and giggling into the wee hours. It'll be fun for you!"

Grandpa's calloused hand rested on Nana's shoulder and he leaned in to kiss her wrinkled cheek. "They'll be fine! These girls don't see one another nearly enough and to think we've got them for a month!"

Nana turned her head and her eyes glistened, patting his hand with her own. "Our last summer before it's gone. It's hard to believe that the land will be filled with condos!"

Aunt Cynthia relinquished her arms from Julia and leaned back against the countertop, her manicured hands spread wide as she leaned forward, looking at her parents. "I can't believe it either. Are you sure, you're making the right decision? The farm's been in the family for generations, Dad." Her eyebrows rose high and she shook her head. "I have a hard time picturing you retired, let alone living in the city—even one so small as Kingston."

Grandpa snorted. "It's not New York..." His gaze flashed to Emma, "...or even Ottawa, but it's the right size for us!"

Grace gave a short laugh and she stepped close to her mother. "I can't picture you growing up here, Mom. It's hard to reconcile with the way you are now—always so busy at the office." She slipped the dark glasses up so that they crowned her head like a tiara. "Did you really feed the chickens and..." Her fingers curled, making quotation marks, "...slop the hogs?"

This time it was Grandpa who chuckled. "Did she tell you that? We never let her do farm work. We had Frank and another hired hand. Nope. We wanted her to get an education and make something of herself." He pointed to Emma and Julia. "Your Dad too, y'know." Turning back to Cynthia, he continued. "Neither you nor your brother ever looked back." His smile was warm and proud when he gazed at his daughter. "Both of you have done well."

"Will you stay and have supper with us, Cynthia? Why not spend the night and head out in the morning?" Nana smiled and walked over to her daughter. "We'd love to have you, you know."

Cynthia slid her hand into her mother's. "I can't, Mom. I'm catching a flight back in a couple of hours." She glanced at her watch. "If I catch the 3:30 ferry, I'll just make it. But I'll spend a few days at the end of the month when I come for the girls. We can catch up then. I just want to pop out to the yard and say hi to Frank before I take off." She fingered an odd looking stone pendant hanging from a leather necklace and smiled going out the kitchen to the back door.

Nana looked over at Grandpa and smiled wistfully. "She still wears it, I see. That's good."

Grace sniffed and her chin rose high in the air, smiling sweetly at her Grandmother. "I don't know why she does. The thing is hideous. She can certainly afford something nicer. But that ugly rock... it's like a fixture with her."

Grandpa nodded. "Aye. For sure she can afford to wear diamonds but she likes that amulet." He exchanged a look with Nana before turning to face the girls. "It's so good to have you all here. I want to hear all about the past year and how you did in school. After Grace and Lily get settled, we'll have some cake and ice cream. It'll give us a chance to catch up. We haven't seen you since Christmas, after all."

Emma watched her grandfather and her eyebrows knitted together. She'd seen that primitive looking necklace a few times but had never really given much thought to it. Grace led the way from the room, a suitcase on wheels trailing behind her. Emma hid the smile that twitched in the corners of her lips. If Grace disliked the necklace, that was all the more reason to admire it. Grace was such a snob.

It was puzzling though that Aunt Cynthia made a point to say hi to Frank. In all the times that she'd visited the farm the hired hand had hardly ever said a word to her or Julia. With his lumbering size and the perpetual scowl dragging his mouth down, his dark eyes alert and birdlike, he was kind of scary. He'd be the last person she'd make a point of chatting with if she were Aunt Cynthia.

"What kind of cake did you make Nana?" Julia's chirpy voice broke the spell, bringing Emma back to the moment.

It was just the four of them there now as Lily had slinked off to bring her suitcase upstairs as well.

"Marble. Something for the chocolate fiends and the rest of us too." Nana stepped over and gave Julia a one armed hug before opening the refrigerator and reaching for the cake.

Well, that was one good thing about the summer. Nana was a terrific cook and she loved to spoil them with goodies. Even so, after her aunt Cynthia left it would be the official start of the summer vacation on the farm— a whole *month* with Grace. Emma sighed. Actually, twenty-seven days and twenty hours, but who was counting?

CHAPTER THREE

Emma sprawled lazily on her bed and watched Grace finish hanging up her clothes in the small closet. She still wore the dark glasses perched on her head, like some kind of movie star. As she passed the large window she paused and peered out across the fields covered with hay and wild flowers.

"Look at that house across the way."

"What house?" Emma asked from the bed.

Grace glanced over to her cousin and shook her head. "*That* one, way over there."

Emma got out of bed and stood next to her cousin.

"It sure looks decrepit No wonder Mom told us to stay away from it. It looks like it's ready to fall over." Her arms folded over her chest and she rubbed her hands over her bare skin. "It looks kind of creepy, actually. It's weird but old houses, abandoned like that, always fascinate me. I wonder about the lives of the people who lived there. Why did they leave? How many families called it *home*?" She sighed.

Emma gazed out the window. Funny, but she had never really noticed the old farmhouse before. But then again, she never had the chance to explore the area around the farm; her visits were always just for the day. "Yeah. It is kind of creepy. I'll give you that. It looks ancient." The downstairs windows and door were boarded up while the upstairs windows peered out at the world. Around it the grass was raggedy and long while a lone tree stood like a sentry next to it.

Grace took a deep breath. "I'd love to know the history." She glanced over at Emma and a small smile appeared on her lips. "Someday, I'd like to be a writer." She laughed. "I can't decide whether I want to write like Hemingway or Stephen King. *That place* is definitely in Stephen King territory though."

For the first time, Grace seemed normal—vulnerable even—the haughty facade dropped for a moment. Emma smiled. "Grandpa probably knows about it. We should ask him." When she looked at her cousin, her eyebrows pulled together. "Did Aunt Cynthia ever tell you anything about that house?"

Grace's eyebrows rose and she sighed, a long and soulful sound. "Not really. Just to stay away from it." She smiled, changing the subject. "I wonder what Lily and Julia are up to. If I know my sister, she's probably petting the pigs or cuddling chickens. She's nuts about animals." Her eyes closed and she huffed. "Not so good with people but give her a dog or cat and she's all over that. She wants to be a vet when she grows up."

"Not Julia. Her plans don't include any sort of physical labour. If she can't marry a rich guy, she intends on being a comedian. She's crazy about Melissa McCarthy." Emma's face flushed thinking of the impression her kid sister had done earlier. "She's actually pretty funny when she gets going."

Grace shrugged and looked down her fine nose as she scanned the room with her eyes. With a disdainful look now, she said, "This room is *smaller* than my bedroom in New York. For all of us? And, I suppose we'll *all* have to share the one bathroom in this place. How is that ever going to work?"

Emma could feel her neck muscles tighten. As if a switch was thrown, the old Grace she knew with disdain was back. "Grandpa put in an extra bath last year. It's on the main floor so no, we all don't have to take turns, sharing a bathroom." Nana and Grandpa's house was a farm house, not a *penthouse* suite. She and Julia shared their own bathroom at home and there were two other bathrooms besides that, but you didn't hear her going on about it.

Twenty-seven days, eighteen hours and counting. She turned and walked out of the room, calling over her shoulder, "I'm going down. Nana made a cake and they're waiting for us. They sent me up to help you but I think you've got it covered."

Downstairs, she found Nana in the kitchen slicing the cake into sections. Grandpa sat at the table nursing a cup of tea in his big, gnarled paws. He looked over when he saw Emma and his eyes lit up. "Gracie all settled in?"

Emma sauntered over to him and put her arm over his shoulder, leaning in to give his cheek a kiss. "I think so." There was no way she was going to let on about Grace's snide comment. "Do you need some help with that, Nana?"

The old woman turned and shook her head. "Nope. But you can give a shout out the back door to call Lily and Julia in." She slid slices of the cake on plates she had stacked and smiled as Emma stepped up next to her. She wiped her hands on her apron and turned to face her husband. "Actually this can wait a few minutes. Dan, don't you have a surprise waiting in the barn for the girls?"

Emma's head swivelled to face her grandfather and she saw the twinkle in his eyes.

He rose to his feet, smiling over at her. "Now's a good a time as any, I guess. C'mon." When they passed out of the kitchen he paused at the bottom of the stairs and called out. "Gracie! Come down here, darlin'."

Emma watched as Grace's hand fluttered on stair rail as she came down the stairs, the heels of her princess sandals making sharp tocks with each step. Coming around the newel post, she managed a small smile when her eyes met Grandpa's. "What's up?"

It was Nana who answered. "It's a surprise. I think you'll like it. Your Grandpa's hit every garage sale in the county. He's gone to a lot of effort."

Emma turned to look at her grandmother. There was a note of warning in her eyes. They'd better like the surprise or she'd let them know about it. It was sweet the way Nana was so protective of him.

Grandpa led the way through the family room and out the back door. The red stained barn was about fifty feet away, the wide doors standing open. Next to them, a man with steel grey hair, in faded blue coveralls was hooking up a long flatbed trailer to a tractor. Emma's stomach tightened into a knot. It was Frank. She saw him straighten and his eyes were like a hawk's never missing a thing watching all of them. Would his face crack if he ever smiled?

Julia and Lily appeared from around the side of the barn. It would be hard to tell they were cousins if you didn't know better. Julia was spritely and full of life, always grinning whereas Lily looked like she was ready to take flight any minute, her eyes darting every which way if they weren't looking down. With her reddish blonde hair that hung in limp strands and pale, sallow complexion, her dark blue eyes with the long dark lashes were her one redeeming feature, if she ever dared to look at you.

"Hey! You should see the ducks in the pond out back. They're so cute! One of them has a dozen babies that follow her around everywhere." Julia skipped past Lily, making her way over to Emma. Her dark brown hair was a mass of bouncing curls above her wide grin. She had dressed for the farm that morning in jean shorts and an oversized Ottawa Senators' T shirt.

"Glad you like them. That's going to be a chore you'll like—feeding them grain!" Grandpa chuckled and nodded to the open door. He could barely conceal his excitement. "But first, the bribe!"

"Go on with you! Just admit you liked getting them the—" Nana caught herself short and shook her head. "Oops. Almost gave it away." Her dark eyes danced watching all of them.

"You're right, of course." Grandpa stepped into the barn and beckoned for the girls to follow.

Emma sneaked a peek at her cousin Grace. The older girl was choosing her steps carefully, avoiding any loose questionable dirt, while her nose was wrinkled with pinched nostrils. The barn smell of the animals and manure wafted heavy in the sultry air.

When Emma stepped inside, her mouth fell open in a grin. Four bicycles were lined up, leaning against the low barrier of the first horse stall. The second biggest, the one she knew was intended for her was purple. "Wow! Thanks Grandpa! How did you manage to get my favourite colour?" She grabbed the handlebars and wheeled it out the doorway and into the sunshine.

Behind her she could hear, Julia. "Grandpa! Thanks!"

Emma turned her head and watched Grace pull the biggest bike, the pink one, from the wall. The corners of her lips curled in a smile that didn't extend to her eyes. "Thanks Grandpa. Where's the gear shifters?"

Nana took a step over and her eyes were cool. "There aren't any. You'll just have to make do like the rest of the girls."

Grace nodded slowly and then looked down at the bike, the streamers hanging from the handle bar suddenly very interesting to her.

Grandpa was on a roll with the bikes. He helped Lily with the last one, a yellow one. "If the seats or handle bars need adjusting, Frank will help you with that. He knows where all the tools are. "

Emma's leg rose and she straddled the bike. There was no way she was asking Frank for any help. When her behind rested on the seat and she was able to touch the ground with her toes, she grinned. She wouldn't need his help. Good.

Grace wheeled her bike next to Emma's and then a genuine smile flashed on her face. "We'll be able to explore!" She turned to face Grandpa when he appeared next to Lily. "Grandpa? That place across the field looks kind of neat, in a spooky kind of way. I'd like to check it out, up close. What's the story—"

"STAY AWAY FROM THERE!" Grandpa's dark eyes had narrowed, staring back at Grace. He glanced over at Frank, and the two men exchanged a silent gaze for a moment. Grandpa sighed and looked down at the ground, his face dark. "You can ride to the village, explore the lanes, go to the beach but that house...that's one place that's out of bounds for you kids."

Emma could only stare at her Grandpa silently. She had never heard him raise his voice to her or anyone for that matter. He was always cheerful and smiling. This was something he really was in a knot about. Her face tightened but she could only wonder what it was about the place that had him so angry. It was just an old house that looked like it could fall over with the first gust of wind.

Nana spoke lightening the mood. "Don't worry. There's lots of great spots to explore without going over to the Hanson place. It's dangerous to set foot in there. You might get hurt, going through the floor or something falling on you."

Grace's voice was softer when she spoke. "I didn't mean to upset you, Grandpa." Her cheeks were flushed when she looked up at him.

Before he had a chance to say anything more, Lily pushed forward and she looked up at Nana. "Can we ride to the beach now?"

Emma's head pulled back staring at her shy cousin. Lily had tried to ease the tension and get past this. She obviously felt sorry for her sister and was uncomfortable with the situation. Still, it had taken some gumption to speak up. More than Emma would ever have given her credit for.

Nana stepped over and placed her hand on Grandpa's arm, patting it gently. "Not now, dear. I've got a surprise for you in the kitchen. How does cake and ice cream sound?"

Julia and Lily spun around and took the bikes back to the barn. They were half way to the house by the time that Emma balanced her bike against the low wall. She glanced over at Grace who was setting her bike to the side. Two pink spots still showed on Grace's cheeks and her lips were a straight line.

Once more, Emma surprised herself that there was a leaden lump in her stomach feeling sorry for her older cousin. Grace had only mentioned the old house but Grandpa acted like it was such a big deal. "C'mon Grace! We'd better hurry or our sisters will eat all the cake."

Grace rolled her eyes and sniffed. "Who cares?" Her nose wasn't quite as high in the air on the walk back to the house. Grace wasn't used to getting yelled at. Actually, neither was Emma.

The old house across the way was a real sore spot with their grandfather. It was something they'd have to put out of their mind and definitely avoid the subject with him. But knowing this, was like trying to not picture a blue elephant after someone told you not to think of it. If she felt that way, what was Grace feeling?

CHAPTER FOUR

At supper, Grandpa was back to his usual cheery self. He looked at each of them in turn, affection shining through from his weathered face."It means a lot to us to have you girls here for a month. I only wish we'd done this sooner. It's sad that it took us this long." He shook his head. "It took selling the farm to think of this."

Emma felt her throat grow tight and she swallowed hard to fight the sudden sadness that rose in her chest. Grandpa had to be almost seventy. She remembered other visits when he'd been a lot spryer. Now, he walked more slowly and sat down more. Frank was probably the same age but he was in better shape, despite the slight limp when he walked. If not for him, Grandpa would probably have sold the farm long before this. It had to be hard on her grandparents changing from a lifetime working the land.

She glanced over at her Nana. Her hair had gone completely white in the past few years and she looked a lot more frail than she'd ever seen her. Her hands were still steady but they were mottled with age spots and her fingers were thin and bony. But still, even though she was more stooped, her eyes were bright and she was usually smiling.

Nana shook her head and she looked over at Grandpa,

sighing with a smile. "Family. That's the most important thing. Remember that girls. You should get to know each other better. Someday...well, you might need each other. We'll be long gone."

"Let's not talk about that. It's too sad." Julia pushed the peas around her plate, trying to hide them under her slice of beef. "I'm looking forward to playing in the hayloft." She looked over at Lily. "We can make a fort or jump from the rafters."

Lily nodded and her eyes were bright watching Julia. "That would be fun. And the animals..." She grinned.

Grandpa chuckled and sat back in his chair. "Speaking of animals..." He looked at each of them and winked. "I think it would be good if you did a couple of hours of chores in the morning and then had the afternoon and evening to do whatever you want."

Emma's gaze flickered between her grandparents. They had this all planned out, not that she minded helping with the chores. Grace looked like she had stepped in dog poo from the set of her lips, but Julia and Lily were eager.

Grandpa leaned forward and reached across the table to pat Grace's hand. "Don't worry, dear. It's nothing horrible like shoveling manure or feeding the pigs. Just a bit of weeding the garden and helping your Nan with the dishes and clean-up." He turned to Lily and Julia. "Since you two like the chickens and ducks, it'll be your job to feed them." He glanced over at Nana. "Nothing hard about it, just adding some structure to the day."

Emma chuckled. The apple didn't fall far from the tree. Her Dad was the stickler about chores at home. "I don't mind. Julia and I are used to making our beds and cleaning the mess in our rooms. Gardening is new, but we can learn how to do it." Emma glanced at Grace again and the corners of her mouth twitched in a smile. Grace's manicure and polish were going to take a beating working in the dirt.

Grace inhaled slowly and her chin rose looking at her Grandpa. "I suppose we can. But what will that hired man do, if we do all the chores? I mean you pay him and you don't want him sitting around with nothing to do all day." She sat back in her chair and smiled sweetly...the kind of sweet that was anything but.

Grandpa shook his head and smiled. "Frank, you mean; his name is Frank. Don't worry about him. He's got plenty to do. And even if he didn't, I'd still never part with him. He's not just a hired man, Gracie. He's my friend. I owe a lot to him."

Grace pulled her head back and rolled her eyes. "I can't see what you would owe him. Thanks to you, he's got a job, and a place to live, especially at *his* age. What will he do when you leave?" She picked the napkin from her lap and dabbed the corners of her mouth.

"He'll be all right. Wherever we go, there'll be a place for him. I owe him my life." The smile had fallen from his lips and he looked down at his plate for a few moments.

Emma sat forward on the edge of her seat. "How's that Grandpa? What happened? Tell us the story."

He shook his head and his eyes closed for a moment. "Never you mind." He looked over at Grace, tapping the top of the table with a fingertip. "Just stay away from that Hanson farm. There's plenty to do without nosing around over there."

Emma sat back, her mind a million miles away from Julia and Lily chattering about their plans for the next day and her Nana getting up to start clearing the plates. She rose and took her plate to the sink. Whatever was up with that Hanson place, it had something to do with Frank. Why else had her Grandfather mentioned it right after talking about his friend?

***

Later that night, Emma sat propped up in bed, sending a text to her friend Ginny about the day. She looked up when the door to their room opened and Grace walked in. She was dressed in a blue night shirt, her fingers clutching a towel and her toothbrush. She stopped in front of the window and looked out into the dark sky.

She spun around and her eyes were wide when she beckoned for Emma to join her. "Quick! Come see this!"

"What?" Emma's eyebrows pulled together and she slid out from the warm cocoon she'd made of the bedclothes. She glanced over at Julia and Lily nestled on the highest bunks and then tiptoed over to join her cousin. She leaned in close to Grace and whispered, "What is it?"

Grace grasped her arm and pointed out the window. "Look! There's a light on over there! Isn't that house supposed to be abandoned?"

Emma leaned forward and looked across the fields to the old farm house. Grace was right; there was a light shining from the old farm. It didn't make sense, not after what Grandpa and Nana had said. "There's someone there! Someone must be living there. But why would Grandpa..." Her eyes lit up. "Maybe someone broke in. Some bum or squatter or..." She gasped. "Maybe they're doing something illegal, like growing dope or something."

Grace squeezed her arm. "Maybe the place is haunted! Grandpa probably knows that and that's why he doesn't want us over there!"

Emma jerked back. "Noooo. You actually believe in that stuff? There's no such thing as ghosts and haunted houses." She shook her head. "I think he's scared of us getting hurt, that's all. The place looks like it's falling down."

"Then why is there someone there with the light on, if that's the case?" Grace looked back through the window. "There's more to this than Grandpa's letting on. I'm going to find out what that is."

Emma's mouth fell open. "But we can't! He was really fired up about us not going over there." She looked back out the window trying to see any sign of movement in the house. This didn't make any sense.

Grace folded her arms across her chest and her chin rose. "Grandpa doesn't have to know if we go over there and check it out."

"*What?*" It came out louder than she intended. Emma

looked over at the still forms of her sister and Lily. Thankfully, they were still sleeping.

Grace leaned closer and her voice was barely above a whisper. "Tomorrow afternoon. We'll head to the beach but detour when we're out of Grandpa's sight. We'll sneak over there and just have a look. We don't have to go *in*, just see what's up with it."

The back of Emma's neck tightened and she scowled. "I don't know. What about Julia and Lily? We can't take *them*!" There was no way she wanted her impulsive sister anywhere near the place if it was dangerous.

"We have to! Lily won't say anything. She's just like me when it comes to spooky stories. How about Julia?" Grace's mouth was a tight, determined line.

Emma turned and looked at the lump in the top bed that was Julia. She'd have to keep an eye on her but..."She's okay. She won't tell. But I don't like this, sneaking behind Grandpa's back. You've got to promise me one thing, first. We don't go inside! We just ride up to the driveway and go no further!"

Grace held her hand up and crossed her fingers. "Scout's honour! I promise, we just look around the outside."

Emma turned and slipped back into bed. Despite the fact it was a warm summer night, she felt a chill skitter up her spine. Part of her hated the fact that she agreed to sneaking over there to check things out, going against her grandpa's wishes, yet...something was going on and she wanted to find out what that was. Maybe they'd be heroes if there was something illegal going on and they told their grandfather about it.

CHAPTER FIVE

Footsteps in the hallway roused Emma awake. Opening her eyes, she looked around in the room, disoriented in the dim light. She tensed before remembering she was at her grandparents farm. That must be them going downstairs.

She sat up in bed and looked around the room. Through the window, threads of pink hung low on the horizon. She turned her head to look at the clock radio on the dresser to see it was only 5:10. She blanched. The sun wasn't even up and her grandparents had already started their day?

Oh boy.

The call of nature cancelled the idea of rolling back under the covers. She thrust the coverlet back and stretched before inching herself up and out of the warm nest. The sound of soft snores filled the air around her sister, while the other set of bunk beds showed her cousins sleeping soundly. She tiptoed across the floor and grabbed her robe hanging on a hook.

After finishing up in the bathroom, she walked softly down the stairs. All her life she was never able to go back to bed after her feet hit the ground. Besides, the smell of frying bacon made her mouth water.

From the hallway she could see Nana, already fully dressed in a flowered blouse and dark pants, standing at the stove, cooking breakfast.

Entering the kitchen, she stopped short and her eyes widened. Grandpa and the hired hand Frank were already eating at the table, with Frank at the head, watching her with inscrutable eyes. This was the first time she ever saw the man in the house, let alone sharing a meal. Up until then, he had always kept to his trailer at the end of the fields whenever her family had come up for a visit.

Grandpa looked up from the set of newspapers he was reading and looked over the top of his reading glasses at her. "Good morning Emma! How'd you sleep?"

"Hey Grandpa. Good, thanks." She circled the table in the center of the room to her grandmother. "Hi Nana. Something smells good."

Nana smiled at her. "Help yourself to juice or milk. One egg or two?" She stepped over to the cupboard and took down more plates.

Emma took her time getting a glass and then filling it with milk. From the corner of her eye she could see Frank take a forkful of egg and chew it, still watching her, sphinx like. When she turned, she nodded at him and murmured a 'good morning', to which he tilted his head. She sat next to him at the table, opposite Grandpa. Even so, she was too aware of Frank watching her. It was like he could see right into her, knowing every secret she'd ever had.

Grandpa lifted his coffee cup. "I'm afraid, the forecast is rain for this afternoon. Bad for you girls, but the hay could sure use it."

Damn. That killed the plan to go swimming or exploring around the old abandoned house, although she wasn't sure postponing the house visit was such a bad thing. The light she and Grace watched last night was sort of spooky. But then, maybe there was a good reason for it?

"Grandpa?"

He looked up from his paper. "Yes?"

"Last night I saw a light shining in the window over at that old farmhouse. I thought you said it was deserted." Under the table her fingers twisted the fabric of her terry robe.

Grandpa and Frank exchanged a silent gaze. The smile had fallen from his face when Grandpa answered her. "I'm not saying I don't believe you...but it must have been some trick of the light...maybe a reflection of the moon or something, because the Hanson place is empty. It's condemned, even." He shook his head. "I wish to hell the township would just tear the bloody thing down."

Frank dropped his fork on his plate; it made a dinging sound. "Was the light on the ground floor or up higher?" His voice was hoarse.

Emma's head jerked to look at him and her mouth fell open. It was the first time she'd ever heard him speak in her life, and he wanted to know about that light? He didn't think it was a reflection, that was clear. "Higher," she replied. Like the second floor or something."

Nana set a plate of bacon and eggs on the table before Emma with a clatter. She stood with her hands on her hips and let out a loud sigh. "Well?" She scowled at Grandpa, then at Frank. "Are you going to check that out? There shouldn't be anyone over there."

The room went silent. Frank kept his eyes on Emma while Nana and Grandpa had a stare down. Like a shroud, the air in the room became thick with tension. Finally, Frank pushed back from the table and rose to his feet. "I'll see to it, Abby," he said in a deep, low voice. He brushed by Nana and left the room. After a moment, the back door banged shut.

Nana, lips pressed together, shot another look at Grandpa and then turned to go back to the stove.

Emma plucked a piece of bacon from her plate and looking down she chewed it slowly. What the heck was up with that? Maybe if she got Nana alone, she'd find out more.

One thing she was certain of though...Grace would find *that* interchange pretty interesting.

***

Emma didn't get a chance to get alone with Grace until almost noon. The two girls were upstairs in their bedroom making the beds and tidying up while Julia and Lily were outside feeding the chickens and ducks.

Grace stood at the rain spattered window pane, looking over the fields to the old house. "Someone's over there! I can see someone walking around the yard!"

Emma tossed the pillow back up onto the freshly made upper bed and wandered over to her cousin. "It's Frank. He's checking the property."

When Grace spun around to face her, her dark eyes were narrow. "What? Why do you think that?"

Emma tiptoed over to the bedroom door and closed it softly. Grace was probably not going to be too pleased that she'd told their grandparents about the light. She walked back to the window to stand next to her cousin. "I asked Grandpa about the light we saw over there at breakfast. He tried to pass it off as an illusion but Frank and Nana were pretty interested, especially when I told him it looked like it was coming from the upper story. Nana was upset so Frank volunteered to go over to check it out."

Grace's eyes widened as Emma spoke. She leaned into Emma and gripped her arm. "*See?* There is something weird about that place!" She turned and peered out the window again. "I'd love to see it. I just know it's got to be haunted or something." She sighed and with an exaggerated roll of her eyes, "It might be the *only* redeemable thing about this summer vacation."

Emma could feel her jaw muscle clench and she blurted it out before she could stop herself. "Do you have to be such a bitch? It's their last summer here and they wanted us to be part of it! Can't you think of someone else besides yourself for once?"

The door opened and Nana stared at them. From the set of her tight mouth and narrow eyes she wasn't pleased. "Girls! What's going on in here?" She pierced Emma with her gaze. "Emma Baker! What would your father think hearing such language?"

Emma felt her face redden. She stayed silent.

Turning to Grace, Nana said, 'The only redeemable thing, Grace? Is that how you really feel coming up here to visit us?"

Grace's mouth snapped shut, and she looked away while her own blush tinged her cheeks.

Nana stepped into the room. "I heard you both when I was halfway up the stairs! What if your Grandpa or Frank heard you? They're right outside you know."

Grace's face turned towards the window again. "No he's not. We can see him over at that old farm from here." Her blush fading she turned her head back to Nana. "What's the story about that place, Nana? We know it's not just that it's old and falling down. Someone is in there and you sent Frank to find out who."

Nana grimaced but she stepped inside and closed the door behind her. "All right. I can see you're not going to leave this alone." She folded her arms over her chest. "But if I tell you the truth, you have to promise me that you won't let on to your grandfather."

Emma and Grace shook their heads and in unison, "No, we won't tell him. Promise."

Nana held up her finger, stopping them cold. "And *for the love of God*, you *won't* go over there!"

Emma barely breathed watching her grandmother. This had to be really good for her Nana to say that, to take the Lord's name in vain. She nodded.

"Okay then." Nana sighed and then looked over at them. "It's one of the oldest houses on the island. There's a sad and tragic history to the Hanson place." Nana stepped over and eased down on Emma's bed. "The family lived there for a few generations before they fell on hard times. The rumours are that the father got involved with some bad people. It was the time of prohibition in the States. There was a lot of money to be made in running liquor across the border. There was no prohibition in Canada, of course."

"I've heard about that. The people doing it were Rum

Runners." Emma had a history teacher who often went off the curriculum telling exciting tales to spice up his classes. She glanced over at Grace who was standing spellbound, listening to the story. This was the sort of thing that was right up her alley if she was interested in becoming a writer.

"Yes. Well, the father, Gerald Hanson, was involved with that, back in the 1920's." She looked at both girls. "Back in those days, the money in bootleg liquor was enormous, like drug dealing today. And just like drug cartels today, those people back then were evil and violent."

Grace's eyes sparked. "Violent?"

Nana nodded. "Yes." Lifting her arm, she pointed at the window. "The entire Hanson family was murdered one night back in 1929."

"WHAT!" Grace's head snapped back to face out the window. "A whole family?"

Emma felt repulsed by the eager look on her cousin's face.

"Yes," said Nana. "It was long before my time, but people here thought that it was some sort of gang war or something." She shook her head slowly. "But it never really made sense to me. They were all poisoned except for the mother, and she was found hanging in the parlour. If it was gangsters sending a message, why would they try to make it look like the mother poisoned her own family?"

Emma was horrified. "She poisoned her family? *Her children?*"

"Oh my God!" Grace pulled a chair over and flopped down in it, next to Nana. "The family died there? And not just that but were murdered! So the place really *is* haunted?"

Nana's voice was soft with woe. "Nobody knows the truth. Maybe she *did* kill them because she went crazy or something, or maybe some murderers did it and made it look like she did it." She shook her head again. "Nobody knows..." She shook her head and looked down at her lap. "But to kill your own children..." She sighed.

She looked off and was silent for a few moments. "When I was a girl in the 1950's something happened there to a boy we went to school with. Allen Croft. He went inside and fell down the stairs. He died there." She took a deep breath and her face became soft. "Your grandfather and Frank had seen him headed that way on the day Allen died. It was thanks to them that the search parties checked it out. It was a tragic thing to happen."

Nana stood up and went to the window. "Back in the 1970's a young couple our age bought the place." She looked off to the side. "Karen and Jeremy something or another... They moved in and were going to fix it up." Nana sighed and she shrugged her shoulders. "They left in a heck of a hurry—they left in the middle of the same night they moved in and were never heard from since. The locals stay away from it."

Nana got to her feet like the weight of the world was on her shoulders. "Now, will you stop talking about the place? It has bad memories for a lot of people around here. Allen was a friend of your grandfather."

She wandered over to the door and opened it, standing there for a beat and turning to face them. "It's funny. I've always felt that we're kind of the sentinels to the place, living just across the field from it. We just don't want any more people getting hurt or..." She shook her head slowly. "Just leave it *alone*, girls. And if you're done in here, you can come down and help with lunch."

Grace popped out of her chair and her voice was light. "We're almost done! We'll be down in ten minutes, tops."

When the door closed and Nana's footsteps could be heard on the stairs, she spun around and there was a wide smile on her face. "That seals it! I *have* to go over there! I'm going to take lots of pictures and write the story! Maybe I'll even get published."

Emma felt a coldness deep in her gut after hearing this, and seeing the excitement in Grace's eyes. "Are you *nuts*? What part of 'don't go over there', did you not understand? She *trusts* us, Grace. We can't."

She rolled her eyes and turned her back on Emma, plucking a hoodie from the closet. "Fine! You stay here if you want, but

I'm going to check it out."

Emma's eyes were like dinner plates. "Now? You're going there, *now*?"

Once more, Grace did her customary eye roll and she shook her head. "Of course not *now*, idiot. I'll wait until the time is right and then I'll go." She shoved her arms into the light blue jacket and sauntered out of the room.

Emma frowned and slumped off after her cousin. Should she tell Nana? Her grandparents had arranged this visit to bring the cousins closer and there she was now, willing to rat her cousin out. That sure wouldn't help. She'd have to find a way to discourage Grace from going over there. Especially now that she knew of the all the people who had died there. Grandpa was right. The place was dangerous.

CHAPTER SIX

The next day dawned better than the one before, weather-wise. When Emma rolled out of bed and looked out the window, the sky was overcast, but at least it wasn't raining. She peered across at the Hanson house, her eye drawn to it like a magnet. Everything was quiet over there. Even last night when she'd checked for the light before falling into bed, it had been still and dark. Maybe Frank had found people hiding there and had run them off.

She grabbed her robe and was about to leave the room when Julia sat up, rubbing the sleep from her eyes.

"Emma?"

She took a step closer and put her finger across her lips signaling to speak lower. Her two cousins were still sound asleep and she had no great wish for Grace to wake up. She'd had enough of her the previous evening, sulking around and being snippy to Julia and her.

Emma leaned close to her sister's face. "What?"

"Do you want to ride our bikes to the village this afternoon, just you and me? I don't mind if Lily comes but..." She looked over at the lower bunk where Grace was huddled into a ball sleeping soundly. She stuck her tongue out and pulled a sour face.

Emma smiled and whispered, "We'll see. Are you getting up?"

Julia threw the covers back and rolled over to rest her foot on the small ladder. She popped off the bed as silent as a cat.

The two girls left the room and Julia disappeared into the bathroom.

Emma could hear the voices of her grandparents drifting up from downstairs and the smell of coffee was in the air. She crept softly down and paused at the bottom step to try to hear what they were saying.

She was able to make out Frank's low, raspy voice "No, none Abby. No sign that anyone had broken in. All the boards were still on the downstairs windows and the doors."

"How 'bout the gate? Was it shut tight?" Grandpa wasn't good at keeping his voice low.

"Look Dan...even if they do go over there, they can't get through the door or windows. We both know what that light was. I'll keep an eye on the place, don't worry." Frank's words were punctuated by the clatter of his coffee cup banging against the table.

It was the perfect opportunity to tell her grandparents about Grace's plan. Yet, Emma held back. Maybe Frank would catch Grace in the act and that would be that. He was always watching with those black hawk eyes of his. One thing she knew for sure, she wouldn't want to be Grace if that happened.

She backed up the stairs and then made a noisy show of coming down again, her feet clattering and yawning loudly. In the kitchen, Nana and Grandpa had plastic smiles while Frank remained, as always, stone faced.

"Morning Em! How are you today?" Grandpa got up from the table and grabbed the coffee pot to top up his cup and offer a refill to Frank.

Emma kissed her Nana on her cheek and then turned around to smile at him. "Fine!" She poured milk and then looked over at her grandmother. "Julia wants us to go into the village this afternoon on our bikes. Is it okay with you?"

Her grandmother nodded and looked past Emma to the doorway where Julia had appeared. "Maybe Grace and Lily would like to go with you. It's a fair ride there—almost two miles."

Julia managed a wan smile and her gaze flickered to Emma.

Words weren't necessary to convey her disappointment. It looked like her plan to ditch Grace for a while wasn't going to work. Emma sighed and then took a seat at the table. Once more she murmured a low 'good morning' to Frank.

The old man turned his dark eyes to her and nodded. He always looked so stern and serious with heavy lines pulling the corners of his lips down. He finished the rest of his coffee, rose and as he strode across the room called over his shoulder, "Thanks for breakfast, Abby. See ya out there, Dan."

Julia picked up the empty plate and mug and set it in the sink before flopping down in the seat that Frank had left. She turned to Grandpa, "He sure doesn't say much, does he? Does he talk to you, Grandpa, when it's just the two of you? Have a conversation even?" She sat back as Nana placed a plate of pancakes and sausage in front of her and Emma.

Grandpa smiled and patted her hand. "Yes, but I agree he's no chatterbox. It works for us. We've known each other since we were your age. When you know someone that long, you can almost read each other's mind."

Julia nodded and poured syrup over her pancakes. She grinned up at him. "It's hard to imagine you, let alone Frank, as a kid. Did they even have bicycles back then?"

Nana let out a whoop from where she stood rinsing Frank's plate in the sink. "Bikes were invented before cars, Julia! We're not that ancient!"

Grandpa reached over and his hand mussed the hair on the top of Julia's head. "You think you're funny! Just for that I ought to make you clean the pigpen and slop the hogs with Frank!" He laughed and looked over at Emma. "What do you say? Should we make her do that?"

"Yuck! The pigs stink so bad and Frank kind of scares me. Yeah, for sure, Grandpa. Julia should have to do that. I'll take a picture even!" Emma laughed seeing the grimace on Julia's face before she popped some food in her mouth.

Grandpa smiled. "You two remind me of your dad and aunt when they were your age, teasing each other."

It was like a light bulb going off in Emma's brain. Her

father! Of course he was raised on the farm! Why hadn't she thought of this before? He probably knew all about the Hanson house having grown up here. She'd call him later and see what she could get out of him about it.

***

After lunch that day, Emma and Julia got their bikes from the barn. They were riding up the dirt path to the house and driveway when Grace and Lily emerged from the back door.

"Where are you two going?" Grace slid her dark sunglasses over her eyes and looked up at the sky which had been clearing steadily all morning.

Lily looked like she was about to cry seeing Julia setting off without her. She wore an over-sized green T shirt and spandex shorts that only served to highlight her spindly legs. "Can I come with you?"

Emma's heart went out to her young cousin. "Of course. We're just going to the village to get an ice cream or soft drink. It's just something to do to break up the day." She smiled when Lily perked up and raced off to the barn to get her bike.

"I suppose, I'll come along too. I'll just finish putting sunscreen on, and be right with you." Without waiting for an answer Grace spun around and went back into the house, her long pony tail of blonde hair swaying imperiously over her shoulders.

"I don't remember asking her to come with us." Julia sneered over at Emma and her toe kicked at the dirt while she straddled the bike.

"Shush! Lily's coming." Emma turned and smiled at her young cousin. "We're waiting for Grace. She's gone to put sunscreen on."

Lily rolled her eyes and stood with her bike propped up against her hip. It was the first time Emma or Julia had ever seen Lily communicate any annoyance at Grace. It felt good to have an ally, even her.

She rolled her bike closer to Julia and murmured. "She's

probably getting changed as well. She wouldn't want anyone to see her in just a shirt and shorts. I bet any money, that she'll come back in a skirt and silk top."

"Why? It's not like we're going to a Broadway play or something. It's just the village store." Julia giggled and pantomimed plumping a hair-doo, holding her nose high in the air.

Lily burst out laughing and Emma couldn't help but notice how pretty she was when she did that. It was like the sun appearing from behind a cloud. Lily's eyes sparkled and her cheeks flushed pink beside a perfect set of white teeth. Even her gold, unkempt hair seemed fairy-light and free.

"Careful, you two. She's going to be back in a minute. She might catch you." Emma sidled closer to the other two girls, watching the door.

Sure enough, when Grace appeared, her lips were glossed and her hair was combed and flowing loose over her shoulders. In a white set of shorts and silky red top, she could have stepped off the cover of a magazine. She was definitely over the top for a visit to Sloan's Country Emporium.

Julia and Lily shared a look and then both looked down at the ground to hide their grins.

"What?" Grace pulled the glasses lower on her face and looked over the rim at the rest of them. "Just because I've got some class..." She lifted her glasses and her chin, taking small mincing steps in the princess heeled sandals going to the barn to get her bike.

Julia nudged Lily with her hand. "Which class is she talking about, second or third?" She turned and shook her head, chuckling and watching Grace.

Even though Emma smiled, she cautioned, "Enough, you two. Be nice." She turned and watched Grace mount the bike and ride up to them, passing them with a small fluttery wave of her hand. The kind of wave Emma had seen videos of the Queen make.

***

When they finally rode into the village, Grace wasn't quite as poised and regal as she'd been when they set out. Her hair was limp, hanging in damp strands and beads of perspiration rolled down the sides of her face. Emma could identify with the feeling. The day had turned muggy with not a breath of air to cool off from the long ride. All of them were hot and sweaty.

They parked their bikes alongside the two story frame store and then ambled around to the front of the building. Emma fanned her forehead before noticing the two teenage boys with cans of soda, sitting on the platform running the width of the building. They turned their heads, watching the girls approach.

Emma's breath hitched in her throat. The guy closest had ice blue eyes and a carefree brush of brown hair, kissed with gold at the ends. When his lips spread in a smile, she felt her face flush. He rose to his feet, his white T shirt showing tanned muscular arms and slim, jean fitting snugly on his long legs. From the looks of him, he was probably a couple years older than she was.

She couldn't help smiling back and turned to glance at the other guy who was still seated. He had the same set to his eyes and mouth but looked even older. He was probably sixteen or seventeen. That one's attention was firmly on Grace as she sashayed by.

"Hi! You girls visiting the island?" It was brother number two, directing his question at Grace.

She paused and stepped closer to him, smiling down. "We're staying with our grandparents, Dan and Abby Baker. Do you know them?"

Brother two rose to his feet, towering over Grace by a good four inches. He nodded and extended his hand. "I'm Barry Morton and this is my kid brother, Mike." His fingers laced through his hair and he looked down for a moment smiling. "We're islanders."

Grace was all poise when she introduced herself and then turned to add, "This is my sister Lily and my two cousins, Emma and Julia."

Emma couldn't help sneaking glimpses of Mike. He nodded and threw a shy smile her way.

"Can we go in now? I'm dying of thirst." Julia stomped by the others and pulled the screen door of the store open wide. Lily scurried behind her, looking down, folded into herself.

"We'd better go in. I've got the money and well..." Emma's voice was almost a croak and it didn't have anything to do with the long ride and how parched she was. She smiled at Mike and then stepped away following the other two.

Her heart beat a little faster as she walked over to the cooler of drinks where Lily and Julia stood, basking in the cool air wafting out. Behind her, she could hear Grace's footsteps. She grabbed a soda and held it to her forehead, closing her eyes for a moment. The chill of the air conditioned store was nowhere near as good as the icy cold oozing from the can. She needed something to clear her head, immediately.

"They're kind of cute, don't you think?" Grace's low voice was a purr in her throat as she her arm slinked by to grab a cola from the cooler.

Emma looked away. For a second, Kyle's face flooded her mind and she felt her stomach fall. Kyle was the guy she'd had a crush on, like forever. Mike might be good looking, but she wasn't interested. Not really. Okay. Well...maybe a little.

"Yeah, I guess so." Emma nudged Julia and they walked over to the cash to pay.

The store was filled with a hodgepodge of dry goods, touristy things, a fishing and hunting section, greeting cards and even a refrigerated room for beer and wine. It smelled of wood and honey. The woman behind the counter was a well worn, middle aged wraith in a stained blouse and slacks. She took the bill and with a wan smile she shoved a few coins across the counter at Emma.

When Emma emerged from the store, Mike and Barry had moved over to the shade of the awning hanging over the large window. It was obvious they'd been waiting, as both of them pushed off from the window sill that they'd been leaning on when she appeared.

Mike stepped closer to her and his smile again was shy. "So...how long are you staying on the island? We don't live far from your Grandfather's place."

"Until the middle of August. Then it's back to Ottawa for Julia and me. Grace and Lily are here from New York. My grandparents wanted us all to get together for their last summer. You know they've sold the farm, don't you? Well, I mean it *will* be sold at the end of September at least."

He nodded. "Yeah, we heard." He grinned at her. "Word travels fast around here."

Grace and Lily stepped out of the building and were immediately joined by the older brother, Barry.

His grin bordered on being a smirk when he looked at Grace. "So, how you enjoying farm life after living in New York City? Big change, I'll bet."

Surprisingly, Grace dropped her sophisticated air and her smile was kind of flirty when she looked back at him. "For sure! It's kind of fun, actually. The quiet at night is weird but I'm getting used to it." She laughed. "Not to say anything about having a *haunted house* as a neighbour. Now *that's* weird. Do you know anything about the Hanson farm?"

Lily's head swiveled to watch her sister but just as she was about to say something, Barry took the bait, hook, line and sinker.

He sidled closer to Grace and his voice became lower, "I know *everything* about that place. It's creepy all right. A bunch of us went over there one Halloween. You know, a truth or dare kind of thing. I went inside. I was the only one with enough guts to do that." He straightened and his chest puffed out like a peacock.

From the corner of her eye, Emma noticed Mike shaking his head and looking down at the wooden floor with a smile. Obviously, he'd seen his older brother trying to impress other girls with that story before.

Grace stepped closer, leaning into him "Really? Did you see anything odd or spooky? What was it like?"

Barry's eyebrows rose high. "Scary as hell! You know the

history, don't you? A whole family was murdered there and then years later some kid got killed there too!"

"What?" Julia stepped over to Barry and Grace. "What place is this? Can we go see it?"

Emma's shoulders slumped and she sighed. But it was bound to happen, that the younger girls would find out the history of the Hanson house. She turned to her sister, "You've *already* seen it. It's that old house across the fields from Grandpa's."

Julia's mouth fell open and her eyes lit up. "Oh yeah. The one Grace mentioned to grandpa. Are we going to—"

"No. We're *not*. Grandpa has forbidden us to go over there. It's falling down and dangerous. He doesn't want us to get hurt." Even as she said it, she knew there was no way that any of the others would heed the warning. Julia was already sold on the idea, always looking for an adventure and even shy Lily looked like she was about to explode with the thrill of it. As for Grace...well, she'd been just waiting for the first opportunity.

"Yeah, that night was the scariest time I've ever had." Barry's head fell to the side, signalling with a nod for the gang of them to go to the side of the platform where a picnic table with a bright yellow umbrella providing some shade, was perched. He led the way taking a seat and smiling when Grace sat facing him.

"What happened?" It was now Grace's turn to take the bait, leaning forward and staring intently at Barry.

Emma barely dared to breathe sitting next to Grace and waiting for Barry to continue. He seemed to be enjoying all the attention everyone was giving him, pausing and looking at each of them before beginning the tale.

The only one who stood casually to the side was his brother, Mike. He grinned and his hand rose high, fingers fluttering, "It was a dark and stormy night and—"

"Piss off, Mike! You weren't even there, I was. I'll tell it if you don't mind." Barry turned back and his eyes bored into Grace's. "It was actually twilight. It was something a gang of us had talked about doing at midnight but when the day came, we changed it to early evening." He chuckled. "We were brave but not *that* brave."

"So what happened?" Emma blurted. He was trying her patience with all the build-up. Plus, there were no such things as ghosts and haunted houses...right?

He glanced over at her and the smile fell from his face. "We rode our bikes over there after supper. The place is all boarded up and locked now, but at the time it was still open. Anyway, when we got to the gate, the wind made the front door clatter against the side of the house, and with the curtain in the front window flapping through the broken glass like a ghost...well, we kind of lost our nerve."

"Thought you said you went in." Julia snickered and took a long sip of her drink.

His eyes were narrow when he turned to her. "I *did* go in! Will you just wait to hear the story?"

Emma felt her neck muscles get tight at the sharpness of his voice and his harsh scowl at her sister. He didn't know them well enough to take that tone with *any* of them. She glanced up at Mike who bobbed his eyebrows and then looked down at his feet. At least he had the decency to look a little embarrassed by his brother's rude tone.

Grace turned and shot a dirty look at Julia before turning back to Barry. "Go on."

"Well, none of us really wanted to go in...but no one wanted to be the first to turn around and leave either. We just stood watching the house for a while and then Jimmy Hofsteader made the dare." He glanced up at his brother and shook his head. "You know Jimmy...his dad being the rich jerk he is and Jimmy being the big shot as usual..." He turned back to Grace. "He said he'd give twenty dollars to the first guy to go inside the house."

"So you took him up on it?" It was the first time Lily had spoken and Emma spun to face her. Immediately, Lily's cheeks began to flush and she looked down at the soft drink she was cupping with her hands. She looked like she wanted to slip through the seat and disappear.

Barry shook his head and smiled, "It wasn't just the money. The other guys were older and I wanted to show them." He took a deep breath and let it out slowly, prolonging the suspense. "I was all alone walking across that yard. I felt like I was about to enter the gates of hell, shaking like a leaf and hoping like crazy it wouldn't show. But it was getting dark and if I was going in there, I sure didn't want it to be at night."

Emma's eyes were wide and she leaned in, just like the others. A shiver ran down her spine despite the heat of the day. Of course it had to be pretty creepy to do that, walk into an old abandoned house when it was getting dark. You'd never catch her doing something that stupid.

"What did you see when you went in there?" Grace's eyes were the size of golf balls watching him.

He hunched lower over his soft drink and his voice dropped. "The step creaked when I put my foot on it. I just about chickened out right then and there. But I knew the guys were watching my every move, so I kept goin'. A gust of wind blew the door again and it banged so hard against the clapboard, it was like a gunshot. I thought about the dead people... the people that *died* in there. I swear my knees were shaking so bad, I could barely walk through the door, but I did!"

His gaze flickered around the table resting momentarily on each girl. "There was a set of stairs to the left of a long hallway—the stairs where that other boy was killed.

"He was killed on the stairs?"

Barry nodded. "Yeah, they found him at the bottom of them with a busted neck."

All four girls gasped at once.

Barry straightened in his seat. "I stepped over to the staircase and even though it was dim in there, I saw stains on the bottom two. It had to have been his blood. As I stood looking around, there was a big bang like a door slamming upstairs. Then the sound of footsteps above me!"

"No way," said Emma.

Barry's face got dark. "Yeah, WAY!" he spat out.

"Hey, man..." Mike said quietly.

"It's the truth and you know it!" Barry said to his brother.

Julia broke the uncomfortable silence. "Holy cow! What'd you do?" Julia was no longer sneering. She leaned forward and her fingers were white knuckled clasping the soft drink.

He turned to look at her and his mouth fell open for a moment. "What'd you think I did? I got the hell out of there as fast as I could!" He turned back to Grace. "That place is *haunted*. The footsteps and banging doors...it scared the hell out of me. I was the only one there so what else could it have been but their spirits still roaming the place. "

Grace's hands flew to her cheeks and she was almost trembling she was so excited. "That's amazing! I'd love to go in there and take a look, see if anything like that happens." She turned to Emma, "Imagine! Hearing footsteps and all that. It'd be too cool for words!"

"It's like something out of a movie! I'll go!" The words burst out of Lily's mouth and for a moment the shyness she wore like a shell was gone.

Emma barely dared to breathe. This had all gotten out of hand so quickly with Barry's story. Was she the sole voice of reason there? She pictured her Grandpa's face. "I don't know—"

"I wouldn't advise going there on your own." Barry ignored Emma and sat back, taking a long sip of his drink to finish the can off. He was really playing it up, the big shot trying to impress Grace.

Emma sighed. Still...if she was honest with herself, she had to admit she was curious. Julia was right. It was something right out of a novel or scary movie. Who knew when she'd ever get the chance to do anything like it again? Had her father ever gone over there with a bunch of guys on a dare, like Barry? She hadn't had a chance to talk to him yet but now that she'd heard this, she was worried that he would feel the same way that Grandpa did and forbid it. That wouldn't be fair! She could just bet that her Dad had gone over to the Hanson house when he was Barry's age, for sure! Even so, it would be best to avoid the topic when she spoke to him later that night.

Anyway, what could it hurt to just go there, stand at the gate or even get close to the house? They didn't have to go *inside*. She looked over at Julia. Her sister's eyes were like marbles, popping out on her cheeks it seemed. Even Lily was keen on this, leaning forward, her shyness forgotten.

"Will you go with us? I mean, you've been there and for sure, I want to go." Grace reached out and covered Barry's hand.

In a flash his hand flipped over and he held Grace's fingers. Even though he'd played the story up, hoping to get next to Grace, Emma had to admit that she was also hooked by now.

She turned to Julia and Lily. "You can't tell Grandpa or Nana if we do this. And you two can't go inside. You'll have to stay at the gate and watch. Is that clear?"

"We won't tell, don't worry. When can we go?" Julia looked around the table at everyone.

Grace pulled her cell phone from the pocket of her shorts and peered at the small screen. "It's too late to go now. By the time we get back Nana will have dinner started. How about tomorrow afternoon?"

Barry looked up at his brother and smiled. "We could be finished our chores at noon if we get an early start. What do you say?"

Mike shrugged. "Sure. Why not?" He looked at Emma and a small smile flashed on his lips. "We can meet up with you there after lunch."

Any second thoughts about going over to the old Hanson farm that Emma might have had vanished when Mike looked at her, his smile warm and friendly. It would be okay if they just took a peek. Besides, Mike would be there along with his brother. What harm could come of it as long as Grandpa didn't find out?

CHAPTER SEVEN

After Emma waved goodbye to her grandfather the next day, the ham sandwich and milk she'd had at lunch felt like a congealed mass in her stomach. A few times that morning she'd toyed with the idea of calling it off, even telling Nana. But in the end her curiosity and the prospect of seeing Mike kept her silent, complicit in the plan to sneak over to the Hanson house from the beach front. She was just as bad as Grace when it came down to it; both of them lied about their plans and sneaking around. That realization didn't cheer her.

She pedaled hard to catch up with the other three, skimming past Frank who stood in the back corner of the yard next to his trailer. She could feel his eyes bore through her and she forced a smile, trying to shed the suspicion that he knew what they were up to. She was probably giving him too much credit. It was a gorgeous summer day and of course there was every reason in the world that they would be going to the beach to swim and cool off. She was probably just being silly, thinking he knew.

At a bend in the path, her sister and cousins disappeared behind the fields of hay and barley swaying in the breeze. Thank goodness they had grown as high as they were; they had a better chance of not being seen by Grandpa or Frank when they cut across the far side of the field to visit the Hanson house.

When she rounded the bend, the rock beach and lake came into view. Julia stood next to her bike looking back and beckoning for Emma to hurry up. Grace and Lily walked their bikes along the edge of the grass before the rounded stones of the beach started. Emma looked back where they'd come from and blew a sigh through pursed lips. The top of Grandpa's two story house and the roof of the barn were just barely visible from the beachfront. There was no way their grandparents would be able to see them. Besides, they'd be too busy with chores to pay them any mind.

"Wait up!" Emma pushed the bike faster to catch up with Grace and Lily.

Beside her, Julia wore a grin. "Did you bring the phone to get some pictures? I can't wait to tell Jessica and Sophie about this! They'll want to see pictures."

"No! You can't tell anyone about this, Julia! If you tell them, they'll tell their parents and pretty soon Mom and Dad will know." Sometimes Julia didn't think things through. Emma stared long and hard at her sister. "Dad would be mad about this. I just know it."

Julia sighed. "Okay. You're no fun but you're probably right." Her eyes narrowed and she edged closer. "How do we know for sure that we can trust Grace or Lily? They might tell and *then* it will get back to Dad."

Emma sighed. "That's the chance we have to take." She looked up ahead at her cousins. "We don't have to do this if you're worried. We can always go back to the beach and go swimming." Even though she'd miss seeing Mike and the creepy house, at least it would be honest. Plus, she wasn't entirely convinced now that Julia would be able to keep the secret.

"No way! This is a lot more fun that swimming. Besides, we can do that tomorrow." Julia grinned and raced ahead before Emma could answer her.

Grace and Lily let their bikes fall to the side and then started walking away from the waterfront through the field of tall grass. Julia was right behind them, the grass tugging at her legs as she hastened to keep up. The plan was to double back towards the Hanson house along the beach and then cut across.

Emma took a deep breath and hurried along. The day was bright with not a cloud in the sky. Seagulls screamed as they swooped over the water trying to spot fish near the surface. There was hardly a breeze to break the stillness and heat of the day. If they had to pick a day to visit the creepy old Hanson house, this was as good as any they'd be likely to get.

She dropped her bike next to Julia's and ran through the field, trying to stay on the trail of bent and broken grass that the other three had forged. She peered ahead at the old farmhouse, at the tall tree next to it, the branches like arms extending over the rust pitted roof. Whatever coating of paint that once covered the wooden frame showed only in some places, a lighter shade than the greyed ancient clapboard. From this angle, an outbuilding could be seen, crouching low behind the main house.

Emma's eyes flickered quickly over the grass that sprouted in the back yard, wild and raggedy, bare earth showing through in places. After she climbed over the wire fence, entering the main property of the Hanson house the air became silent as a tomb. No bird cries or even flies buzzed in the fetid air; it was as if they were warned to keep away.

"This place is seriously creepy." Grace's voice was barely above a whisper when she peered over at Emma. The four girls stood close together, near the fence, poised to bolt at the first odd sight or sound from the house.

"Do you think Mike and Barry are here yet?" Julia sidled closer to Emma but craned her neck to see around the house to the front driveway.

"They're not here." Lily's voice was flat and her eyes were wide circles staring up at the second story window.

The hair on the back of Emma's neck tingled when she gazed at Lily. What was up with her? It was like she was in a trance or something, staring at the house. Her tone of voice had the ring of certainty, totally unlike her normal, hesitant self.

"C'mon. Let's go around to the front." Grace led the way,

keeping close to the fence, while her eyes were trained on the house. Her hands clasped her arms below the shoulder and she rubbed her bare skin briskly, even though the day was hot.

Emma brought up the rear as they walked single file. A couple of the upstairs windows were broken, the shattered glass looking like a spider's web clinging to the frames. The downstairs ones were boarded up, hiding the macabre secrets, guarding the inside from intruders. Though the gingerbread trim was missing in places, the swirls that were left clung like bats to the peaked soffits on the under-hang of the roof. Scanning the building, she guessed the house had four or five bedrooms from the size of it. But now, the only residents were probably spiders and mice...creepy enough, in and of itself.

"Oops! Sorry!" Julia jerked back from where she'd bumped into Lily.

Lily had stopped, standing stock still, squinting up at a dark window. She stepped closer to the house, still peering intently.

"What? Did you see something?" Emma's heart beat fast in her chest. She looked where Lily was staring, trying to see what it was. There was only a stained curtain caught on a shard of glass in the otherwise dark hole in the house.

She took a deep breath. This was eerie, yes, but she was probably getting spooked out by the stories she'd heard. It was only a house after all. Sure, people had died there but that happened in lots of old houses way back when. Lots of people probably died at home. That was life. Right?

Lily stepped back to the fence. "No, I guess not. But it looked like someone was there for a moment. Just from the side of my eye I saw something move." Her mouth was set in a straight line as she hurried to catch up with her sister.

Julia turned and her eyebrows bobbed high gazing at Emma. The usual smile was gone from her face. She was as puzzled and uneasy as Emma was with the house and Lily's odd behaviour.

Grace stood at the gate at the end of the driveway focusing her cell phone to take a picture of the front of the house. Lily had been right. Barry and Mike were nowhere to be seen.

Emma stepped close to her sister and stared at the boarded up door and the front step which was weather beaten and slanting low at one side. It wouldn't take much for the whole step to tear away from the house if someone walked on it. This was starting to feel like a really bad idea. She glanced over at Grace. "Now what? Should we leave?"

"What do you mean? The guys will be here soon. We're probably early." Her pink glossed lips curled in a sneer before she strode away, walking closer to the house. She held the phone up, pointing it at the upper floor getting photos from different angles. "If those walls could talk, huh?"

"So much pain and fear..." Lily spoke softly gazing up at the second floor windows. "That's the story they'd tell. Those poor children. What could be worse than dying at the hands of your mother?"

Emma's head swiveled and she stared at her cousin. "How did you find out about that?" Barry hadn't said anything about the mother killing her kids. Even Nana hadn't been sure that's what happened.

Lily turned and there were tears in her eyes. "Can't you hear them? The whispers in the air...their voices?"

Emma felt a chill go down her spine like a million ants skittering on her skin. She couldn't say anything for a few moments as she stared at Lily. She shivered and then took a deep breath. There had to be some explanation for Lily knowing about the family. Probably Grace had told her what Nana had said.

"I don't hear *anything*. Even the cicadas are quiet." Julie looked over at the tree and then around the brush growing at the other side of the property. "You'd think there'd be at least a crow or two. There's always birds at a farm, right? But here, there's nothing."

"Hey there!" It was a deep voice coming from behind, down the long laneway.

Emma spun around. She felt her muscles relax seeing Barry and Mike pedal up the road, stopping short on the other side of the gate. Mike flashed a smile at her before shrugging the straps of his knapsack from his shoulders. He set the bike on its side and strode forward.

"Sorry, we're late." Barry pushed the gate open enough to slip through and ambled over to where Grace stood. He was also carrying a knapsack.

"That's okay. We haven't been here long. I've been getting some good shots of the place." Grace watched Barry reach in his knapsack and bring out a small pry bar. "Good. I'm glad you thought to bring that."

He smiled and winked at her. "Just like the boy scouts... be prepared."

Emma sighed and then looked up at Mike. "We're really going to do this, I guess." When he nodded, she looked over at Julia and Lily. Julia's face was pale and she clutched the wire fence with white knuckles but Lily looked kind of dazed, looking up at the upper story of the house. Emma stepped closer to the two girls. "You two stay here. We'll just take a quick look and then we'll be right back."

She turned and walked slowly over to the front step to join Grace. The squeal of nails giving up their hold in the wood pierced the quiet when Barry reefed on the pry bar. The high pitched noise went straight through Emma's core and she covered her ears with her hands.

Barry tossed the wide board onto the grass behind him and turned to begin on the next one. "Almost got it," he said as he began pulling at the bottom edge of the board. With a grunt he yanked on the board but this time, instead of coming cleanly away, it split in two. His knuckles snagged across the wood and he yelped, dropping the pry bar. He shook his hand, splattering drops of blood over the step.

Emma's gaze flew to meet Grace's. This was a bad sign. Grandpa had warned them they'd get hurt and already it had happened. "Maybe we shouldn't do this."

Grace scowled and shook her head. "Don't be silly. The board was rotten, that's all." She reached into the pocket of her jean shorts and handed Barry a tissue. "Here you go. That'll have to do until you get home."

Mike stepped by Emma and picked up the pry bar from the step. "Here. Let me have a go at it." He wedged it into the crack between the board and the door frame and gave it a sharp yank, pulling the broken piece of wood away.

"Frigging board! I've probably got splinters an inch deep!" Barry held his hand up. Red began to spread through the white tissue wrapped around his fingers. His mouth was a tight line until he looked at Grace and his expression thawed.

"Are you all right?" Julia called from the fence, fifty feet away.

Grace turned and motioned with her hand, dismissing her cousin's concern. At the thud of the board falling Emma peered past Grace and saw Mike stand back and shoot a grin of satisfaction her way waving the pry bar like a trophy. Her stomach was a tight hard knot watching the door and Mike's efforts. In a few minutes, he turned and tossed the last of it away.

"Ready?" Mike waggled his eyebrows at Emma.

Her heart beat fast looking at the scarred wooden door. Even if she didn't believe in all that supernatural stuff, it was still a scary prospect, going in there. What if they fell through the floor? But she knew that it was more than that. Face it. The place was seriously creepy. She crossed her arms and shivered for a moment.

Grace gave her a look bordering on contempt and stepped by Mike. She grabbed the door handle and turned it, pushing the door open wide. Dust motes floated, catching the light in the dank, musty air. A rotten smell of decay drifted into Emma's nostrils and she grimaced. Once more Grace raised her cell phone, although it was hard to say if she'd get any shots. The place was almost totally dark, except for the beam of light shining down the stairwell from the upstairs window.

Emma followed closely on Mike's heels. He had taken a flashlight from his back pack and held it low, so they could see better. She kept her arms crossed, her hands rubbing her upper arms for warmth. It wasn't just the damp chill in the house that made her cold, it was knowing the horrifying history. She peered at the landing in the stairwell, seeing the dark stain there that Barry had described the day before—the place where her grandpa's friend had died.

Her footsteps were slow and careful going forward to the archway where Grace had stepped through. Mouldy woodwork and patches of stained plaster showed through the walls, made her recoil from brushing against it.

"That's wierd." Grace's voice broke the silence. "What's a milk can doing in the living room?"

Emma, still clutching her arms tight to her body, stepped through the archway, her eyes drawn to where Grace was taking pictures. She almost jumped out of her skin when Barry spoke.

"Wait till you see the kitchen! The plates are still on the table! Just like the last supper!" He had gone through towards the rear of the house.

She grimaced at his words before once more, gazing around the room. The fact that the furniture was still there made the house creepy enough, let alone dinner plates left on the table! Grace slipped by her, to join Barry at the back of the house.

Emma was standing just inside the doorway. Mike touched her arm gently. "How are you doing? Are you okay?"

"F...fine," she lied. She turned to follow Grace to the back of the house. She just wanted to get this over with and get back out into the bright sunshine, where she could breathe better. The air felt thick, like it was lying against her skin and she shuddered.

Barry shone his flashlight around the dim kitchen, highlighting the plates on the table and the pots still sitting on the stove.

"This has been here since the 1920's!" he said. "Shouldn't it look... I don't know... messier or something?" The beam of his flashlight played over a half loaf of bread and a bowl of what had to had been mashed potatoes that were on the counter.

"That's crazy, Barry," Emma said. "Even if it was in the refrigerator, it would be covered in mold in just a few weeks." She had gotten in trouble at home last Fall when she stashed a slice of pizza at the back of the fridge and forgot about it until it started to smell two weeks later.

It was hard to see everything. Only spears of light pierced through the boards covering the window, leaving the far corners deep in shadow. When Barry's flashlight roamed over the room, she was able to see the stove and an over-turned wooden chair. Layers of dust and dirt coated every surface. Spider webs floated from the ceiling and clung to every piece of furniture.

"Shine the light on the table so I can get some pictures." Grace held her cell phone up and a series of bright flashes of light sliced through the air. She nodded to Barry as she moved around the room aiming the cell phone camera, following the beam of his flashlight.

All the while Emma stood stock still, hardly breathing watching her cousin. Hopefully this ordeal would be over soon. It wasn't just the dirt and decay, there was an uneasiness in the house, like they were being watched. A couple times she glanced to the side, sure she'd seen something move, but found only still shadows.

"Let's see the upstairs!" Grace pocketed her phone and then grasped Barry's arm, tugging him along beside her for the light.

Mike must have sensed Emma's unease because he slipped his hand over hers, pointing his light on the floor so they could see where they were walking behind the other two.

"Thanks." Emma's voice was a hoarse whisper when she looked up into his eyes. The look he shot her, nodding showed a silent tension. Why were they even in there? Their intrusion was disrespectful as well as downright scary. *People died here!*

Even Grace and Barry were hushed, their feet slow and quiet as they walked up the old stairs. The creaks of the wood were like low groans as they climbed.

At the top step, Emma looked down a narrow hallway where three doors on each side gaped open. The windows on that floor were uncovered and it was easier to see with the daylight shining in. An ancient threadbare carpet ran the length of the hall and cobwebs crouched in the corners high above. Grace and Barry slipped through the first door to the left and Emma looked up at Mike, nodding to the other door, the one on the right.

She sighed. Tufts of gray stuffing and horse hair protruded from the torn striped fabric of a slim mattress, hanging askew on an iron bed frame. From the stained and faded wallpaper of pink roses, it looked like the room was used by a girl— probably a girl, the same age as she was. Her shoulders slumped lower. How sad.

Emma wandered over to an ebony wooden dresser where a hairbrush and comb still sat on the top. The hairbrush was tarnished black with a few silver swirls in the design of the handle peeking through. Her hand rose and as she was about to touch it, a resounding 'No' reverberated in her head. She drew back quickly, staring at the hairbrush while her fingers tingled. What the...

"Ready?" Mike cleared his throat and turned, to leave.

It was enough to bring her back to the present. "Yes." She took a deep breath and followed him down the hall and into another bedroom, this one larger than the first. There was a double bed and two sets of dressers and a wardrobe.

"This had to be the parents' room, don't you think?" Mike walked over to the far wall and opened a narrow door. He shone the flashlight inside. "Hmmm...not much in here, just an empty closet."

Creak!

Emma spun around, looking through the open door. "What was that?" It had come from the stairway. Her heart was in her mouth!

Mike's blue eyes were rimmed with white as he strode by her. "Who's there?"

Grace and Barry were just coming from the first room when Emma stepped out into the hallway. She looked spooked out as well, with her fingers fluttering low on her throat.

"It's just us. Sorry. We wanted to see inside." Julia led the way up the stairs, no longer trying to be quiet about it. Behind her, Lily was white as a sheet, her eyes gazing quickly around.

Emma's jaw tightened. "I told you to stay outside! Go back!" They'd scared the hell out of her! And she was the one who wasn't supposed to believe in this supernatural nonsense! And the way Lily was acting...so quiet and strange, this was the last place *that* girl should be.

Grace shook her head and looked over at Emma. "Let them stay. Not that we can stop them anyway!" She turned and her eyes were mere slits staring at Julia and Lily. "But be careful! Stay together and make sure you're in our sight...well at least on the same floor as us, okay?"

"They'll be fine! C'mon, let's check out the next room." Barry reached for Grace's arm, leading her down the hallway.

"This is spooky, isn't it? I mean, it was awful outside but in here..." Julia's eyes were the size of marbles when she reached the top step. She jerked her head to the side, indicating the first room from the stairway. "What's in there?"

"It was the Hanson girl's bedroom. Her name was Irene."

All three of them turned to gape at Lily. Her voice had been low but the quiet assurance in it, made the hair on Emma's arms spike.

"How do you know that?" Emma eased forward, standing closer to Mike and watching Lily. "Grace told you about the family, didn't she?" But that still didn't explain how she knew the name, Irene?

Lily shrugged her shoulders and there was a forlorn expression on her face. "I just...know. As soon as I stepped inside the house, it came to me." She stepped by Julia and then went inside the first bedroom.

Julia leaned into her sister, whispering softly. "That was weird."

"Totally." It was out of Mike's mouth before Emma had a chance to say anything. "Let's check the rest of the upstairs and then get the hell out of here." He turned to walk to the last room on the side of the hallway they'd started with.

When he stepped inside, his voice rose, "Holy shit!"

CHAPTER EIGHT

Emma's hand tightly gripped Julia's arm. She practically dragged her sister to the last room where Mike had gone. There was no way she was letting Julia out of her sight.

"What is it?" Emma spoke though Mike's back was to her and he was looking down at the floor on the other side of the room. She hurried over and stood close to him, following his gaze with her eyes.

She jerked back with a gasp. A scattering of toy trucks, tin soldiers and blocks sat on the floor near the window...but it was the doll in the torn gingham dress, the blue eyes open staring blindly at her, that sent a shiver up her spine. The blonde hair was in dirty tufts, showing a pink flesh colour of scalp in places. The mouth of the doll was wrong. It gaped wide at an angle that showed it'd been smashed and torn, never to close again. It looked like it had seen all sorts of horror...or been party to it.

She almost jumped out of her skin at Grace's touch on her shoulder.

"What did you find?" Grace edged by her and looked down at the doll. "Gross! Imagine having that thing as a toy! Dressing it and playing with the horrible thing. I'd never sleep a wink."

"No kidding!" Barry had joined the group.

Mike bent forward to pick it up and Emma snapped. "Don't!

Leave it alone!" It was the same feeling that'd she'd had with the hair brush. This stuff was bad. She didn't know why or how she knew it, but she did. "Let's get out of here." She spun around and started for the doorway. They shouldn't be there.

THUD! THUD! THUD!

Emma jolted back and her breath caught in her throat. The floor under her feet vibrated with the force of the bangs. Her heart thundered fast in her chest and she froze to the spot.

"*What the hell was that?*" Barry crouched lower, looking like he was ready to race out of there at any minute.

"Emma?" Julia stepped over to the doorway, her eyes and face panic stricken. She clutched her sister and held her hand. "What was that?"

It was enough to spur Grace into action. "Lily! Where are you?" She shoved past her cousins and Barry, racing out into the hallway. She heaved a slow sigh. "There you are...thank God."

"It was the front door. It banged shut. We're not supposed to be here. Now we're trapped." Lily's voice was soft and without expression.

Barry stepped out into the hallway. "What do you mean, we're trapped? We're not—"

BANG! Followed by the sound of breaking glass.

"Shit! What was that?" Grace pulled Lily's arm, bringing her sister close.

"Let's get out of here! Hurry!" Barry's feet thundered on the stairs. Grace pulled Lily along, following him quickly.

When Emma stepped forward a flash of silver seemed to protrude out of Lily's back pocket for a second. But there was no time to give it any thought as she and Julia scrambled to the stairway. When she rounded the landing and could see the front door, Barry was yanking on the handle, trying to pry the door open. The muscles in his tanned arm strained. His other hand hung limp at his side, the blood staining the tissue thoroughly.

"Here! Let me help!" Mike raced by Emma and Julia, running down the rest of the stairs and over to Barry. He shoved his brother aside and his hands closed over the knob.

Emma's heart was in her mouth watching him work at the door, lifting his foot to brace it against the frame while his arms were tight tendons pulling on the door handle. Beside him, Barry held his hand before his chest, the tissue wrapping his fingers started to drip blood. Oh my God! This was a nightmare!

She stepped down from the last stair, her arm around Julia, holding her tight to her body. "Hurry! We've got to get out of here!"

"What about the back door? Maybe we can kick the boards away." Grace clutched Barry's arm and urged him along the hallway to the kitchen.

THUD! THUD!

Emma squealed, gripping Julia tight. It was coming from upstairs now! They were trapped! Mike turned at the sound. Sweat rolled down the side of his face and his eyes were like dinner plates.

"Hurry! Just get us out of here!" Julia turned her face into Emma's shoulder, Her shoulders shook as she cried, clinging to her sister. "Oh God, why did we come in here?"

"GET BACK!" The heavy growl came from the other side of the door.

Oh my God! It sounded like Frank! It was the sweetest sound Emma had ever heard. Help had arrived!

"Emma? Grace? You girls okay?" Her grandfather sounded frantic.

"Grandpa!" Emma and Julia leapt forward, pounding their hands against the door. "Help us! We're trapped!"

Emma turned at the sound of fast footsteps racing down the hall. Lily stood silently next to the stairs dumbstruck while Grace ran down the hall past her. "Grandpa! Help us!" She slapped the door with both her hands. "We can't get it open, Grandpa!"

"Stand back! We've got a sledge hammer! We're going to beat the door down." Again it was Frank's voice, strong and steady.

Mike and Grace stepped back and he gripped Emma's arm tugging her and Julia back past the stairwell.

The door shuddered at the pounding of the heavy hammer. Emma huddled Julia's head beneath her arm and looked up the stairwell. Whatever had banged around up there was quiet...for now. Something strange had made that noise. She shivered picturing what it could be from all the spooky movies she had seen. The house *really was* haunted. What else could explain it?

At the sound of splintering wood, Emma turned. A shaft of light shone through the hole in the door next to the handle. After more hearty thuds, the door fell open and Grandpa was framed in the bright sunlight outside. He looked scared to death, his leathery face drawn tight with worry.

Julia was the first one through the door, rushing into his arms. "I was so scared, Grandpa! It was coming for us!"

He patted her head, holding her close and his gaze at Emma, looking over Julia's shoulder, brought tears to her eyes. He'd been so right about the house! If only she'd had the sense to listen to him. She rushed over to him and his arm circled her shoulders.

"Come on! Let's get going, Lily!" Grace sounded frantic.

Emma turned and looked back through the doorway. Grace was tugging at Lily who moved like she was in some kind of a daze. The poor girl was scared to death, like a deer in the headlights. Behind her cousins, Mike and Barry edged forward, doing everything but shove the girls out of the way.

Grandpa leaned forward to clasp Grace's arm and then reach to fold Lily to his chest. "Thank God, you're all right."

"I'm sorry Grandpa." Grace had tears in her eyes as she stepped by him and went down the steps.

Frank's voice was choked up and low. "Not half as sorry as you could have been. Believe me."

CHAPTER NINE

Later, back at the farm, the girls huddled on the sofa in the living room while their grandfather paced in front of them. Emma had never seen him this angry. His hands clenched and unclenched and his eyes were fierce chips of blue grey steel, scowling at them.

"It's all my fault, Grandpa. I wanted to see the place. I kind of bullied the others into going with me." Grace's voice hitched and her fingers rolled constantly over and over one another.

Hearing Grace, Emma's head swiveled to stare at her. She was actually willing to take the heat for this? She would never have given her cousin credit for doing anything noble. Up until this moment she always saw Grace as self centered and selfish.

Emma's shoulders dropped lower and she sighed. "No. That's not entirely true. I went along with her. But Julia and Lilly aren't to blame. Please Grandpa, don't punish them for our mistake."

"Mistake! No, it wasn't a mistake! I told you not to go over there and you deliberately disobeyed me!" His eyes were narrow, sparking fire when he looked at Grace and Emma.

Emma sat still as stone, wishing she were anywhere else but facing the wrath of her grandfather. Julia reached over and held her hand.

Nana had been standing just inside the doorway. She stepped forward and put her hand on Grandpa's arm. "Dan, they're just kids. And—"

"Exactly! Kids! They could have been hurt!" His hands covered his face and dragged slowly down and he shook his head. When he looked at them again, his face was haggard and lined. "Or worse. If anything had happened to you, I couldn't live with myself. Now you know why I was so set against you going over there, don't you?"

Julia leaned forward. "For sure. It really is haunted! There were loud bangs upstairs and then the door slammed shut and wouldn't open! I thought we were goners! Thank God, you showed up when you did."

"Thank God and Frank." Nana's voice was hushed, unlike Grandpa's when she spoke. Her chin was lowered and she looked up hesitantly at her husband.

He huffed a short sigh. "You know of course that I have to punish you. You're grounded for the rest of the week. No beach, no riding the bikes to the village. You'll stay in our sight until we know that we can trust you again. AND...under no circumstance are you to ever go over to the Hanson farm again."

"You're not sending us home?" Emma's felt her face loosen and a smile begin. If someone had told her a few days ago that she'd be happy to stay on the farm with her cousins, she would have said they were crazy. She sneaked a glance at Grace and Lily. Grace's eyebrows bobbed high, but Lily was still in kind of a dazed state, sitting there quietly.

"No. I probably should but I'm not going to. I'm so thankful, you got out of that...that horrible place in one piece." He slumped down into the chair across the room from them and sighed. "As for those boys...I'll have to give their father a call later. They should have known better than to go over there."

Emma leaned forward. "But what about Dad and Aunt Cynthia? When they were growing up, didn't they ever sneak over there? Dad's never mentioned the place to me."

"Cynthia and James knew to never go against their father, although Cynthia sometimes pushed the envelope. But as far as the Hanson farm goes, she was deathly frightened of it. I never knew why in particular, but her being afraid of it was enough for me. She never went over there. Not as far as we knew." Nana's voice trailed off and she sighed.

"It's got something to do with that necklace she wears." Lily surprised everyone when she spoke softly. Her eyes met Emma's and then she looked down at her hands.

"That ugly thing?" Grace sniffed, about to say more but Emma cut her off.

"How do you know that? Did she tell you something?" Emma stared at Lily. There was more to this that her young cousin knew. She'd acted so strange ever since they'd set foot at the Hanson farmhouse. It was still affecting her.

Lily looked up. "Just that Frank gave it to her. It was some Native thing...kind of a talisman, something for protection. That's why she warned us not to go over there. She must have sneaked onto that farm, when she was young." Lily's eyes were dead and her voice was a flat monotone.

Grandpa and Nana exchanged a look but neither said a word after Lily finished. Emma watched them closely. This had come as a surprise to them. Maybe only Frank knew anything about that. He'd given Aunt Cynthia the odd looking necklace for a reason.

"We're done talking about that place. Suffice it to say, the house is evil and should be torn down." Grandpa got to his feet and once more his face was set in stern lines. "You girls can stay in your room until we call you down for supper. I'd like you to think about what you've done today." He stepped across the room but paused before going out the door.

He turned and his eyes were sad. "Maybe you *should* go home, after all. This was a mistake asking you here."

CHAPTER TEN

Emma felt the weight of the world pressing on her shoulders as she trudged up the stairs to their bedroom. Grandpa looked heartbroken when he'd left them in the living room. She could have stopped all of this, if she'd only told her Nana that morning. And she sure could have done without the horrible experience in that haunted house. She'd be lucky to ever get a good night's sleep again after that.

Yes, going over there had been a nightmare in more ways than one. She flopped down on her bed and watched Grace wander over to the window, gazing out at the Hanson farm. Emma shook her head and sighed. "Well, I guess we ruined the summer for Grandpa and Nana."

"Nonsense. He'll get over it." Grace turned and fished her cell phone from her pocket. She stood looking at the photos she'd taken and frowned.

"That's all you've got to say about it?" Julia stood with her hands on her hips, her chin jutting up as she spat the words at Grace. "This is all your fault. We should apologize again, do extra chores! Maybe he'll—"

"It's hard to see these pictures on this screen." Grace totally ignored Julia's outburst when she stepped over to the dresser and picked up her laptop. She sat on her bed and plugged the phone into the side of the computer.

"Oh my God! Can you *hear* yourself? You're still going on about that house and the pictures you took even though Grandpa just about had a stroke over it!" Julia scowled at Grace and then climbed up the small ladder onto her bed.

Emma shivered thinking about how terrified she'd been when they couldn't get out of that house. And those thuds from the upstairs, even though they'd been up there and seen it was empty! From the corner of her eye she saw Lily sidling over to the small ladder on their set of beds and climb up to lay on the top bunk. Lily had been acting strange ever since they'd set foot on the Hanson property.

"Are you okay, Lily?" Emma was about to get up and check on her when Grace's voice stopped her cold.

"Holy cow! Quick! Come here and see this!" Grace's eyes popped wide and the color seemed to have left her face. She sat on her bed with the laptop perched on her thighs, staring at the screen.

Emma stepped over and sat next to her. The hair on her arms tingled and she gasped at what she saw in the picture. It showed a single bed still strewn with bedclothes and darkly stained, but hovering above it was a light, greyish mist. She peered closer. Just barely visible, a young boy's face and form could be seen. "Oh my God!"

Julia pressed in behind her, looking over Emma's shoulder to see. "It's a ghost! Wow! You got a picture of a *ghost* Grace! How creepy is that!"

"Let me see!" Lily scooted over the side of the bed and landed as lightly as a cat on the floor next to Grace's feet. She bent over, pulling her hair back out of the way so she could see the screen. "That's the son. Look at how sad his eyes are." She straightened up and her gaze drifted off to the side. "Joshua. I'm sure that was his name."

Once more Emma's mouth dropped as she looked up at Lily. "How do you *know* these things? You knew the girl's name and now this one!" There was always the possibility that Lily was making it up, trying to impress everyone but that wasn't like her. Being the centre of attention was Grace's style, not Lily's. And from the dazed look on Lily's face, she seemed as surprised by knowing the names as everyone else.

Lily shrugged her shoulders and squeezed in next to Grace, watching the screen with the rest of them. Grace tapped a key to bring up the next pic. It was the kitchen but the lighting was so dim that it was hard to make out the table or anything else in there. No ghostly images invaded that space.

When she tapped it once more, Emma gasped. In the corner of the living room was a woman in floor length old fashioned dress, her dark hair pulled back severely in a bun. Again the shape was diaphanous and lighter in colour than the surrounding walls and furniture. She remembered feeling that she was being watched when she was in the house. Now she knew why.

"That must be her...the woman who killed her family." Julia's voice was a soft whisper. "How horrible. She was a witch."

"For sure!" Grace looked over at her sister. "Lily?"

"Her name was Ida. She was the one who killed them." Lily's voice was flat. When she turned to look over at Grace and Emma, her eyes were glazed and her face showed no expression.

"You're giving me a case of the willies, Lily. I can't believe you know this. How is it possible?" Julia snuggled into Emma, staring with wide frightened eyes at her cousin.

"I can't help it. I don't mean to scare anyone but I heard them, even before we went inside. At first it was soft whispers...but then they got louder and louder until I *had* to listen. It was voices in my head; you guys didn't hear them. Why me?" Lily's eyes welled up with tears and her fingers rose to swipe them away.

"It's okay, Lily. Oh God. Now I really feel bad dragging you over there." Grace put her arm around her sister and hugged her close. "I had no idea it would affect you like this. You poor thing."

Emma's throat got tight and she took a deep breath to ward

off her own tears. Yes, poor Lily. And even poor Grace, for that matter, dealing with the guilt and worry. "I think you must have some kind of..." her hands grasped at the air as she groped for the word, "...*psychic* gift, Lily." A cold shiver ran up her spine. "You hearing their voices, and then these... these *things*...to show up in the pictures Grace took..." She hunched her shoulders and shuddered. "It's too weird for words."

"*Now* do you believe in ghosts?" Grace was back to her normal, snotty self, sneering at Emma. "This is going to make a great story. I will *definitely* get it published. I'm gonna be famous." She grinned. "Grace Mullins, Teen Age Ghost Hunter! Maybe I can get a TV show!" She turned back to the laptop and clicked the key again, changing the picture once more.

There was only one other photo that showed anything odd. It was in the bedroom where the doll had been. Despite the clarity of the photo, a dark shadow hung next to the window. It could have been entirely natural; a result of the bright sunlight coming in the room and casting a shadow, but Emma didn't think so. There were no other shadows showing from the light shining in.

She peered closely and then looked over at their window. "That's the room where we saw the light shining last night, Grace." She turned back to the picture and her face grew tight. "Lily? What do you make of that shadow?" She pointed her finger close to the screen.

Lily turned to the screen again. She lifted her hand and brushed the surface lightly. Shaking her head slowly, she said, "I don't know. I don't get a good feeling about it...whatever it is, it's powerful. It controls the house and everything in it."

CHAPTER ELEVEN

At the knock on the bedroom door, all four of them jerked their heads up at once. Grace slammed the laptop shut and then set in behind her. "I don't think we should talk about the pictures to Nana and Grandpa," she whispered. "They're upset enough." She rose and walked over to the door to open it.

Grandpa stood there looking older than ever. His shoulders drooped and he was hanging his head. Keeping his gaze on the floor he said, "It's time for dinner. I think we need to talk." He turned around, leaving them with the sound of his footsteps on the stairs.

Julia got to her feet and her eyes were bright when she turned to face Emma. "Maybe he'll let us stay. I hope so." Her chin lowered, "I feel so rotten about all this. The poor man is heartbroken. Anyone can see that. And it's all our fault."

Emma sighed and stepped up beside her sister. "After what happened over at that place, I think he knows we would never go over there again." There was no way, she'd ever set foot in the haunted house again. Ever! She turned leading the way out of the room, purposely avoiding looking out the window and any sight of the old creepy house.

Grace's eyebrows rose. "Maybe he'll tell us more about it— the Hanson house, I mean."

Emma spun around to scowl at Grace. In the process, she noticed Lily straightening the pillow on her bed. When Lily turned, her gaze dropped to the floor and her cheeks became pink. She looked guilty as sin. Emma sighed. Lily probably felt the same shame that she felt, going against their grandpa's orders and now about to catch more hell for it. Grace on the other hand, seemed totally impervious to shame.

"Let's avoid that subject unless he brings it up, okay?" Emma continued walking out the door and then down the stairs, Julia moving slowly ahead of her.

In the kitchen, Grandpa sat at the end of the table. Emma peered at him, trying to read his face. Had he softened at all? Was he still thinking of sending them home? But if it was poker they were playing, he'd definitely be good at it. Nana moved silently across the room setting a bowl of steaming food on the table.

"Grandpa?" Julia took her seat next to him. "I would really like to stay, honest. Will you let us—"

"That's what I wanted to talk about." He turned to her and his face softened. "It was a foolish thing you kids did. You have no idea..." He looked over at Emma and then her cousins. "I was just so scared for you. I can't take a chance that it won't happen again. The next time might finish you."

"We promise, Grandpa. We're so sorry." Emma looked into his eyes. She looked over to Grace and Lily. She arched her eyebrows and tilted her head, willing them with her eyes to speak up.

"I'm sorry Grandpa." Lily looked down at her plate, speaking so softly, her words were barely audible.

"You have my word, Grandpa." Grace leaned forward and placed her hand on his. Her eyes met his and she even managed a small smile.

His eyes flickered over each of them and he sighed. "Okay. I'll take your word on it. Remember, a person is judged by their word. Don't give it easily." He reached for the bowl of mashed potatoes, offering it to Julia.

Now that things were less tense and he'd relented on

sending them home there was a burning question in Emma's mind. "Grandpa? How did you know we were in trouble over there?" She helped herself to a slice of ham before passing the platter along to Grace.

"Frank suspected. He checked the beach and when there was no sign of you, he came to get me." Grandpa snorted. "There's not much he misses...especially when it comes to that wretched house. He's got some kind of sixth sense about it."

The light in the stained glass lamp hanging over the table began to flicker. It flashed on and off like a strobe light and a whirring hiss, an electrical noise, sounded above them.

"What the..." Grandpa looked up at the light. "Looks like we need a new bulb." He started to get up but it stopped and the light became steady.

Without warning, the radio on the kitchen counter blared a song and Emma jumped.

All of them looked across the room while Nana jumped to her feet and rushed across the kitchen to the counter to press the 'off' button. The silence was deafening. Nana's eyes were wide when she turned to face them. "The switch was already off, Dan."

Shrugging his shoulders and pushing his chair from the table, Grandpa said, "It must have been some sort of power surge." He wiped his mouth with his napkin and got to his feet. "I'd better check the barn. With all that hay and dried wood, it would go up like a torch," he said as he left.

"That's strange," said Nana. "Maybe a car hit a pole or they're working on the hydro lines." She took a seat at the table and her smile was nervous looking around at them. "I'm glad your grandpa changed his mind about you staying. It wouldn't be a good way to end our time at the farm. Besides, I'd miss you like crazy."

Once again, the light over the table began to flash and crackle. Emma looked up at it. Her mouth fell open and a feeling of dread seeped into her muscles. After what she'd gone through earlier, the strange things in that Hanson house, she couldn't help wondering if somehow the two things were related. But that was crazy. Wasn't it?

But when her gaze shifted to take in Grace and Lily's faces, it was apparent from the open mouthed stares at the light, that they were thinking the same thing. This was no coincidence.

"Maybe we should turn it off Nana, before it blows." She went to the wall to flick the switch off.

There was still the light shining from the other ceiling fixture across the room. They weren't in total darkness, which was a relief.

"We could get a candle. Dinner by candlelight. Make the most of this." Grace forced a smile, looking across the table at Nana.

The light suddenly flashed on again and Emma froze. How could that be? Just like the radio, the power came on, all on its own? This was too weird. Things like that never happened. She flicked the switch up and down with no effect.

Lily stood up, murmuring over her shoulder as she walked across the kitchen. "May I be excused? I need to use the bathroom." She passed Grandpa who was coming back in from the barn. He watched her race to the bathroom and shrugged his shoulders. "Well...everything's fine out in the barn."

"Well, it's not *fine* in here. The light just went on all on its own, Grandpa!" Grace's face was pale while she stiffened straighter in the chair, looking as if she was about flee.

Nana set her fork down. "Dan? What could cause that?" She looked worried as well, the lines in her forehead deep furrows now.

He ran his hand through his grey hair and looked down at the floor. "Maybe it's the switch, a short or something. The house is old after all. I'll get the trouble light and have a look at it after supper." He shook his head and his face wore a blank look as he walked back to take his seat at the table.

"But Grandpa...what about the radio? It came on, even though it was turned off. Would the switch there be faulty as well?" Julia turned wide dark eyes to her grandfather and swallowed hard.

Emma and Grace shared a quick look at each other. There was no need for words. The problem with the electricity was beyond odd...especially happening right after the terrifying experience at the Hanson house.

Grace took a big breath and leaned over the table closer to their grandfather. "I took some photos when I was in that house, Grandpa." Her voice was softer when she continued. "I didn't want to upset you more but...the pictures show ghosts— a boy and a woman!"

Grandpa's mouth dropped open and he sat back.

"Does that have something to do with what's happening here?" Emma blurted. She was way beyond caring how Grandpa would take it. Had whatever was in that place followed them somehow? Was it *here*?

"I'm scared." Julia reached under the table and her fingers clasped Emma's.

Grandpa sat straighter in his chair and took a deep breath. "Calm down everyone. I'm sure there's a logical explanation. At least wait until I take closer look at the switch plate and the radio. Let's not jump to conclusions." He held his hands up like a traffic cop, and flashed a look across the table at Nana.

She spoke as if on cue. "You Grandpa's right, girls. Have you ever heard of Occam's razor?" When the answer was blank faces, she continued. "Basically, the right answer to a problem is usually the simplest one. Let's finish dinner and then we'll sort this out. Everything is fine."

Emma squeezed Julia's hand and looked over at her sister to reassure her. Nana was doing her best and there was no point scaring Julia any more until they knew for sure. She looked up when Lily appeared in the kitchen doorway.

"I'm going upstairs to lie down. I don't feel well." Lily's hand rose to tuck a lock of hair behind her ear. Her face was pale and drawn and she looked like she was ready to throw up.

"Would you like some ginger ale or aspirin?" Nana was already on her feet walking across the kitchen to Lily.

Lily looked up at Nana and shook her head. "No. I think everything is catching up with me...being in that house and all."

She slipped away from Nana's arm around her shoulders. "I'll be fine in the morning. I'm just tired."

Nana turned when Lily disappeared from view going up the stairs. "I hope that's all it is. What a day!"

Emma looked over at Grace. "Just in case...would you mind deleting those photos? I don't feel right having them around. I'll hardly sleep a wink as it is tonight without them being in the room with us."

"No! I'm not deleting them!" Grace rolled her eyes and sighed. "But, look I'll tell you what. I'll put them on a jump drive and delete them from my phone and laptop. Then I'll put the drive outside somewhere...maybe in the barn. Would that suit you?"

"It would help." Emma managed a weak smile. "I'll go out to the barn with you later." It was the least she could do since Grace was being so agreeable for once.

The rest of the dinner was quiet. Grandpa seemed absorbed in some inner turmoil, probably trying to figure out the electrical issue. For everyone else, the food was barely picked at before Nana rose and began to clear the table.

***

Emma entered the bedroom ahead of Grace and stopped short. The room had been ransacked. Lily stood next to Julia's bunk, tugging the cover up to re-make the bed. She turned, wide eyed and her face flushed scarlet when she looked at Emma.

"What the heck are you doing?" Emma stepped over to her own bed where the coverlet was a tangled heap, the pillow sitting on top of it. It had been made up and tidy when she'd left it earlier.

Grace stood in the centre of the room, looking around at the clothes hanging from the gaping drawers in the dresser. "Lily? Did you do this? What is wrong with you? I thought you were sick. Why the heck did you make this mess?"

Lily's face flared and her gaze darted everywhere but at

Emma or Grace. "I was looking for something."

"What? Why would you think any of us would have it? What on earth are you looking for?" Grace's jaw set tight and she stepped closer to her sister.

For a moment Lily just stood there, breathing quickly and looking down at the floor. "My...my book." She glanced up at her sister before her words came out in a rush. "I thought maybe one of you hid it on me as some kind of joke."

"Are you *insane*? We've been together all day. And why on earth would we do that? In case you didn't notice, we're all still a little freaked out about what happened today. Believe me! You book is the last thing on *any* of our minds!" Grace bent and lifted her cell phone and laptop from the dishevelled mess on her bed. She tugged the coverlet on the bed and smoothed it before taking a seat.

Emma watched Lily look away and then climb up to her bunk. The young girl was lying. She'd been going through their things but she wasn't looking for her book. Actually, she'd never even noticed Lily reading a book since they'd been here. What the heck had she been looking for?

She took a seat next to Grace and watched as her cousin clicked the keyboard and the photos loaded onto the flash drive. If there was one thing she agreed with Grace on, it was about Lily. The kid had been acting odd all day, being all psychic and saying creepy things. And now, rifling through everything, looking for something. But for what? It had something to do with the Hanson house. She didn't know how she knew, but she was sure of it.

"Lily? What book are you reading, in case I come across it?" Emma listened carefully for the answer.

"Uh...Harry Potter." Lily's answer was soft.

Emma stood up and looked into her cousin's eyes. "Oh yeah? Which one?"

Lily's mouth clamped shut and her eyes became wide. "Uh...I can't remember the title."

"Okay. I'm done here." Grace stood up and jerked her head to the side, towards the door. "Let's get this over with.

Going out to the barn at night isn't something I'm going to enjoy. You said you'd come." She led the way out of the room.

Emma glanced back at Lily and paused for a moment. "If you're not too sick, maybe you can straighten out this mess before we get back." The young girl just stared at her, her cheeks flushing pink again.

What was really going on here?

CHAPTER TWELVE

They went to the barn and stuck the jump drive on a shelf. Leaving it there made Emma feel easier already.

Coming back into the house, they saw Nana sitting at the kitchen table, working on a jigsaw puzzle.

"How is Lily?" Nana held a puzzle piece between her fingers, looking up at Emma and Grace. Across from her, Julia continued to try a piece in a couple of different spots. Grandpa was in his usual spot at the end, holding a mug of tea in his hands and sipping it slowly.

If not for what Emma knew had happened earlier in the day and at dinner, it could have been a heart warming scene of her grandparents and sister. It seemed surreal to her now. How could they just be sitting there doing a puzzle as if nothing had happened?

"She was fine I guess. When we left, she was lying down." Grace looked at her grandfather. "How did you make out? Was it the wiring that made the lights go wonky?"

His eyebrows rose high and he shook his head slowly. "No. It must have been something in the power lines outside. That's the only thing I can figure. I'll check the news report later, in case someone had an accident and hit a hydro pole."

BANG!

Emma jerked back and spun around to face where the noise had come from. A picture lay on the floor, propped against the wall which it had fallen from. A shiver went down her spine and her body stiffened.

Grandpa stepped by her and picked the picture up. The glass covering the print of a basket of apples was still intact. His fingers brushed the wall and he peered at the floor. "Now where did that nail go? It must have slipped out somewhere down here."

Grace and Emma shared a look. This was no coincidence. First the lights and the radio at dinner and now pictures falling from the wall. Even Lily ransacking the bedroom...They'd gotten rid of the photos on the phone and laptop. That couldn't be it.

"Grandpa? Could we somehow have brought a ghost or something from that place with us when we left?" Grace stared into her grandfather's eyes. "It might explain the light flickering and the radio coming on by itself. I've read about—"

"Grace! Stop this. You're scaring Julia." Nana's voice was sharp. Her hand covered Julia's while she scolded Grace with her stern look. For her part, Julia was wide eyed, leaning across the table close to Nana, the puzzle forgotten.

Emma didn't want to believe it could be true but then again she'd never believed in the supernatural until that afternoon inside the Hanson house. "Nana. Julia was there. You can't shield her from this. What if what Grace said is right? What do we do then?"

Grandpa walked slowly over to the table and slumped down into the chair. "If that were true, then wouldn't this house have been affected long ago?" He put his hand to his chest and gazed at his spread fingers. "I was in that place as a boy," he said in a low voice. "I heard those noises back then..." he lifted his eyes. "I saw that... that horrible black...thing."

Nana gasped. "*You never told me that!* You knew Allan had gone there, but *you*? Dan? You were there too, weren't you? You were there inside that house when he died, weren't you?" Nana pressed forward, leaning over the table and her eyes bore into Grandpa's.

Emma and Grace took a seat on either side of him. She clasped Julia's hand in hers under the table. Grandpa looked like the weight of the world was on his shoulders, looking up from under his grey eyebrows at Nana.

"I was." He sighed. "Allen made the dare and he ended up paying the price for our stupidity. If not for Frank...I would have died too."

"What happened when you were there, Grandpa? You said you saw a black thing..." Grace put her hand on his arm, leaning into him. She was eager to hear...so was Emma. "What was it?"

He shook his head slowly. "I don't know... it was like a cloud, but worse somehow. We went upstairs, looking from room to room. Allen wanted to see where they'd died—the family. Then there was a noise downstairs; some kind of banging. It scared the hell out of us at first but then Allen thought it was Frank playing some kind of joke on us. When he went to the head of the stairs..." his face screwed up, "something pushed him! It shoved him right down the stairs! I tried to grab him but I missed!" Grandpa's fingers threaded through his hair as he looked down at the table. "I'll never forget it."

"Oh my Lord." Nana's voice was a soft whisper. "Allen was a smart Alec, but for that to happen...You say he was pushed? Poor Allen."

Emma sat forward. "But that black cloud...what was that? We didn't see anything like that. Thank God. But it was in the photos. The noises and that doll were spooky enough."

Grandpa's eyes were sad looking over at Emma. "It was the ghost I guess. The air was thick... but cold... it went right through my bones. When I ran to the door, it wouldn't open. Just like today. Even the rocking chair I threw at the window...it bounced right off the glass. I thought I was done for."

"But how did you get out?" Grace crossed her arms over her chest, rubbing her hands quickly over the prickly skin there.

Grandpa turned a weary gaze to her. "Frank. He found an old milk can and smashed the window from the outside."

Emma gasped. "Oh my God! We saw that milk can still in there!" She turned when Julia spoke softly.

"So Frank saved you? No wonder you're still together."

Grandpa nodded. "Just like today. It was Frank, again. He knew you'd gone over there." He sighed. "That's why I don't think that whatever is in that blasted house followed you." He looked around the room. "But I got to admit that the lights and the radio are acting strange." He looked over at Nana and nodded.

She seemed to take the cue from him because she spoke quickly. "We'll find out tomorrow what caused it. I'll call the hydro company and have them come to check it out if need be. There's got to be a logical explanation for it. You're not to worry about this, girls."

Emma felt Julia squeeze her hand and she looked over at her sister. There was no way she was going to let her sleep alone until they knew for sure. Who was she trying to kid? Julia wasn't the only one spooked by all this.

CHAPTER THIRTEEN

Later that night, Julia and Emma were in the bathroom brushing their teeth and getting ready to go to bed. Grace had already gone in, leaving the bathroom free.

Julia tucked her toothbrush into the travel case and snapped the lid shut. Tears welled in her eyes when she looked over at her sister. "I've changed my mind. *I want to go home,* Emma. This is too scary. I'm going to call Mom and Dad to come get us."

Emma put her arm around Julia and hugged her close. "I'm scared too, but I think a lot of that has to do with being in that house today. Grandpa's probably right. There must be a logical explanation for what happened at dinner with the lights and radio." Even if she wasn't entirely convinced that it was so, she had to put on a brave front.

She pulled back and looked into Julia's eyes, her thumb rising to swipe the tear from her sister's cheek. "Why don't we see how we feel in the morning? If we still feel the same, we'll call them. There's no sense worrying them now. They can't do anything about it. We'll be fine. You can even sleep with me, if that makes you feel better."

Julia nodded and even managed a small smile. "Okay. But I get the inside, next to the wall. That way it gets you first."

"Just don't kick me, okay?" Emma popped her toothbrush into the holder and opened the door, looking behind her and signalling to be quiet. They tiptoed down the hall, pausing when they heard, Grandpa and Nana's low voices still talking in the kitchen.

When Emma opened the door to the bedroom, Grace stood at the window looking over at the Hanson farm house. She felt her stomach sink as she crept over to her. The sound of Lily's slow and steady breathing, a soft snore, hovered behind her. There was a full moon that illuminated the outline of the house but otherwise it was completely dark. She sighed long and slow at the sight.

"It's still the same. No lights, thank God." Emma turned to cross the room and join Julia in the small bed.

'Yeah. I kind of wish there was though." Grace murmured softly before turning away.

"Not me. I don't wish that." Emma lifted the comforter and climbed into the bed. Beside her, she could just barely make out Julia giving an eye roll and shaking her head.

"But you're not a writer. All of this will make a great story." Her bed creaked slightly when Grace climbed in and pulled the comforter up. "Good night."

"See you in the morning." Emma snuggled closer to Julia. But it would be a long time before she drifted off to sleep.

***

Emma's eyes flew open and she lifted her head. What was that? It had sounded like footsteps walking near the door. She looked over the room but there was nothing or nobody there. A spear of light shining in from the window revealed the dresser and wardrobe hulking against the other wall.

From the corner of her eye she saw movement, a dark shadow flitting across the mirror's surface. Her heart pounded fast in her chest while she squinted her eyes looking directly at it. But again, there was nothing, only the reflection of the beds.

She laid back down and took slow deep breaths to calm

herself. It had been nothing. Perhaps a trick of the light shining in from the window—a shadow of cloud passing over the moon. Yeah, that—

Creak.

She jerked upright again, tilting her head to hear better. The breath froze like an icicle in her throat when the faint creak sounded once more. There *was* someone there!

She could hear the steady breathing of her cousins on the bunk beds next to theirs and Julia's soft snores beside her. It wasn't them and she was pretty sure it wouldn't be her grandparents!

Tugging the comforter higher over her face, she huddled deeper into the bed. Grace's words played in her mind. *'a ghost following them there'*. She swallowed hard and tried to put it out of her mind. It was her imagination...just her imagination.

Creak.

Louder this time...and closer! She became still as a statue, barely daring to breathe.

"Who's there?" Grace was highlighted in the faint moonlight when she sat up in her bed.

Emma's eyes widened. She didn't know whether to be relieved or even more frightened that Grace had heard it too. "Grace?" She whispered.

There was a rustling of the bedclothes and then a beam of light pierced the darkness, illuminating the far side of the room. Grace stood, a ghostly image in her white nightgown holding her cell phone high before her. "There's nothing there, Emma." Her voice was hushed.

A breeze fluttered the curtains bordering the yawning gap of the window. Emma inched out of bed and crossed the room to close it. Grace sidled closer, the both of them peering across the moonlit field to the Hanson farm. A lone yellow light glowed from a window on the second floor.

Emma gasped and her fingers flew to clutch Grace's arm. "Look! It's back!"

"Oh my God!" She turned and looked towards the door. "This, on top of that creaking we heard... I'm going to get

Grandpa. He needs to see—" Grace began to turn but Emma stopped her.

"No! He'll come in and wake up Lily and Julia! It's bad enough we woke up without scaring them too! There's nothing we can do anything about it at any rate, not now. Let's stick together. We'll be okay tonight. We'll tell him in the morning!" Emma looked over at her bed where Julia snored softly. They'd have to go home. There was no way they could stay there with all the weird things happening. Grandpa and Nana would be sad but they'd understand.

Grace sighed and shrugged Emma's hand off. "It wasn't the pictures. We know that now...but I heard footsteps in here. *You did too!*"

At the rustling in the bed across from them, they turned in time to see Lily sit up, her eyes wide peering at them.

"What are you doing?" Lily tossed the coverlet aside and climbed down the ladder. She tiptoed across the room and edged in between them to gaze out the window. "Oh no. What are we going to do?" Her hand went to her chest and she looked down at the floor. "It's all my fault, I—"

"Go back to bed, Lily. Don't worry. Everything will be fine." Grace put her arm around her sister and walked her back to the beds.

The cooler night air and cold floor sent a chill through Emma. Even though climbing into the warm nest next to Julia was tempting, she knew she needed to visit the bathroom first. Grace was just getting back into her bed when Emma opened the door and crept down the hall, quietly.

When she finished and was washing her hands at the sink, she spied an unfamiliar hairbrush sitting on the counter, next to her. Her eyes narrowed. It hadn't been there earlier when she was getting ready for bed, but it looked oddly familiar. Where had she seen it before? She reached to pick it up.

She gasped and whipped her hand away before touching it. It was the hairbrush she'd seen on the dresser at the Hanson house! How had it gotten in her grandparents' bathroom? Her forehead tightened, reliving the visit earlier in the day at that house. A flash of Lily turning and racing to the stairs when they'd heard the banging. There had been a glimpse of something silver in the back pocket of her jean shorts.

Her hand flew to cover her mouth. Oh my God! Lily had taken the thing from THAT place!

Waves of nausea roiled through her stomach as she stood looking at the silver swirls in the centre of the brush, the edges tarnished an oily black. She backed away, never taking her eyes off it, opening the door and slipping out of the room. She stood still for a moment. What should she do? If she told her grandparents, for sure Lily would catch hell. And really, as long as it was in the bathroom, it could wait till morning. There was no sense getting her grandpa all riled up in the middle of the night.

She tiptoed back into her bedroom and climbed into the bed next to her sister, cuddling up for warmth as much as for the comfort of having her safe and next to her. The image of the hairbrush refused to leave her mind. Just as she was about to get up and tell Grace, a loud crash reverberated through the house. She jerked upright in bed.

"What was that?" Grace leapt from her bed and raced to the door.

"Emma?" Julia grasped her arm, clinging for dear life. "What was that? Is it here? That ghost?"

"Stay here! I'm going to see what happened." She pried her sister's fingers away. "Lily? You stay here with Julia!" Her heart beat fast as she stepped onto the floor to scramble after Grace. When she reached the door, she could see Grandpa coming out of his room and tying his robe tight, heading to the stairs. Grace stood at the top waiting for him.

Her grandfather brushed by Grace, moving quicker than Emma had ever seen him. He gestured with his hand for them to stay back and continued down the stairs. Nana scampered out of their bedroom and stood beside them. Worry and fear lined her face as she clutched the sides of her worn red robe tight to her chest. She reached for their hands and her grip was tight.

"It might be a prowler. Although here, in the middle of nowhere..." Her voice trailed off and she leaned over the stairs, trying to hear. "Lord save us."

Emma looked over at Grace, seeing her own fear mirrored in her cousin's eyes. She knew without saying that they were both thinking the same thing. This was all because of their visit to that blasted farm that day.

"*What the hell?*" Grandpa's voice drifted up the stairs.

"Dan? What is it?" Nana hurried down the stairs with Grace and Emma trailing close behind.

When they got to the kitchen, Grandpa was stepping out the other doorway. The sound of him checking the front hallway was followed by a low curse. "The doors are still locked tight. What the devil?"

Emma stopped short halfway across the kitchen. The table was turned over and laying on its side on the wooden floor. An apple and orange from the bowl of fruit that had escaped the broken yellow container had rolled across the room, and a banana was below them. The fruit looked like a face, with the banana making a frown.

Her grandpa entered the room, shaking his head. His hooded eyes met Nana's. "I don't know, Abby. There's no one there."

There was no prowler. *The table had fallen all on its own.* The sight of it made Emma's blood run cold and her heart threatened to jump right out of her chest. "Grandpa! It's that house! There's the light in the window again! And Lily took a hairbrush from one of the bedrooms there!"

Grace gripped Emma's arm. "What? Don't blame her. You don't know that!" Her eyebrows were a straight gash when she defended her sister.

Emma jerked away. "Yes I do! It's in the bathroom upstairs!" This whole situation was Grace's fault! If she hadn't dragged them all over there, this wouldn't be happening! "You're to blame for—"

"Girls! Stop this!" Nana scowled at them, her eyes darting from one to the other. "Get a hold of yourself and help your grandfather lift the table." She nodded her head to the side and then stepped over to help as he bent over to grip it.

Emma bumped Grace's shoulder with her own as she stepped by her. She'd hold her tongue but not for Grace's sake. Her eyes met Grandpa's as she stood next to him, lifting the table to its original spot. The poor man looked like he was about to have a heart attack, his face flushed beet red.

"Grace. You pick up the fruit and the pieces of the bowl. Get another from the cabinet." Nana strode over to the sink and poured a glass of water. "Dan. You'd better take your meds. With all this excitement—"

A high pitched squeal pierced the air. It was coming from upstairs! Emma spun around. Julia! As she ran to the stairs, taking them two at a time, Julia's and Lily's cries for help rang through the night. When she reached the top stair, gripping the newel post to round it, her hand flinched off of it as if she were scalded.

Her eyes were round discs looking down at it. It wasn't heat she had felt, but rather icy coldness. Her breath formed a vapour before her, a white cloud forming in front of her face!

Julia and Lily pounded frantically on the bedroom door, their cries for help knifing through her body. She raced over to the door, vaguely aware of the others also running up the stairs.

The door handle froze to her skin and refused to budge. Even though it was a warm summer evening, the air and door were hoary with white frost.

"Help us! It's so cold! The door shut tight and we can't open it!" Julia's words were mixed with the sound of her frenzied tears. "*Emma! Grandpa!*"

She felt hands tug her away and her grandfather was next to her, shouldering the door and trying to turn the handle.

"Get back! I'm going to break the door down!" He backed up a couple of steps and then charged the door. He cried out as his body bounced off the icy surface. He blinked and took a breath, preparing to hit it once more.

Emma turned away, looking at her Nana and Grace

standing at the stairs. This was no use! There was no way they'd be able to break that door. It hadn't budged a hair! They needed...

"Frank! I'm going to get him!" Emma pushed by Nana and Grace and she flew down the stairs. As she ran through the hallway to the back door, the sounds of the footsteps and creaks in their bedroom earlier filled her mind. Whatever thing had made those sounds in the bedroom was in there now with her sister!

She jumped from the back step to the walkway leading to the barn. Even though the warm air eased the prickles from her cold skin, she barely felt it, hardly noticed the flagstone path under her bare feet. Julia was in trouble! She had to get her out! She bolted by the side of the barn to the end of the yard where a low light shone over the trailer's entry.

Her fists pounded on the door. "Frank! Help us! Hurry!" She pounded so hard her hands tingled with the shock of hitting the firm metal. Oh God! He had to have heard her. Hurry!

It seemed like an eternity before the light in the trailer lit up and Frank's head appeared in the open doorway. His hair hung in long strands next to his stern jaw and his eyes were like dark coals peering down. "What's going—"

"It's Julia and Lily! They're locked in the bedroom and...and...there's something in there with them! A ghost or something! Hurry!" She turned and started for the house again, only looking back briefly to see him shoving his arms in a shirt, as his plaid pyjama covered legs closed the distance between them.

"Where's Dan and Abby?" His voice was a low growl coming awake. He gripped her shoulder stopping her cold.

"He's trying to break the door down! But he can't do it! We need *you*!" Emma scrambled away, once more racing to the house.

When she got to the back door she turned to see where he was. As he came into view she could see his fist curled around a thick handle and the iron sledge above it. Behind her, the sounds of the girls screaming and thuds of Grandpa banging the bedroom door could be heard. "*Quick! Help them!*"

He stepped by her, his legs sure and steady as he rushed down the hall. "Dan? Hold up!" His footsteps pounded the stairs and Emma was just in time to see him reach the top and round the post.

When Emma got there, her grandfather was hunched with his hands on his knees straining for breath. Frank swung the sledge back and was about to slam the door with it. "Step back, you girls!"

THUD!

The heavy iron hammer bounced back as if on a spring. There wasn't even a dent in the surface of the wood. Frank's head jerked back and his face became a tight knot of confusion. He took a deep breath and eased the hammer away, his muscles flexing below the short sleeves of his shirt before once more giving a mighty swing.

THUD!

Again, the hammer bounced away, fast enough that it was wrenched from his grip. It landed with a bang next to his foot. His eyebrows were a tight line over narrow eyes as he gaped at it. "What the devil?" His voice was low and hoarse. He looked over at Grandpa and shook his head. "It won't budge, Dan."

Emma felt her stomach lurch at the eerie wonder in his eyes. Oh God. Her sister was trapped in there!

CHAPTER FOURTEEN

"Oh my God! It's happening again!" Grandpa straightened and the whites of his eyes showed. "The door. The bloody door...*We can't break through it!*"

Grace raced by the two men and pounded on the door with her fists. "Lily! Lily! Are you okay?" Tears rolled down her cheeks and onto the floor. Her hands flattened on its surface and she slumped lower to her knees.

"*Grandpaaaa!*" At Julia's blood curdling scream, Emma rushed forward. The fear that had been in her sister's voice was now terror. "Oh please God, help us!"

"Julia! What is it? Tell me!" Emma's heart was going a mile a minute, standing still as a stone next to Grace and trying to bore through the wood with her eyes.

"*Something's wrong with Lily! She's twitching and rolling on the floor! Help us!*" Julia's voice was pure hysteria now.

Grandpa stepped forward and pausing for a deep breath, his voice was steady. "Keep her from hurting herself! If there's something to put in between her teeth, like a pencil or washcloth, do it! Try to stay calm, Julia. Help her!" He turned and there were tears in his eyes when he looked at Nana and then to Frank. "This is all my fault. I never should have—"

"Dan! That's not helping!" Nan rushed forward and took him by the hand leading him away from the door.

Her grandfather's words echoed in her mind. '*It was happening again...*' Emma took a deep breath and turned to face her grandparents. "It's that hair brush! If Lily hadn't brought it back here, this wouldn't be happening!" She started towards the bathroom but Frank's words brought her to an abrupt halt.

"*Wait!* She brought something back with her? Where is it?" He took a step towards her, towering high, his face a lined mask of anger.

Emma's mouth fell open for a moment and the muscles knotting in the back of her neck loosened. For Frank to be this angry, there *had* to be something to it. "It's in the bathroom—an old silver hairbrush on the counter."

He reached for her arm and then stepped by her pushing his way into the small room down the hall. He emerged after a few minutes and his face was blank. "What hairbrush? There's only a comb and a bottle of hand soap. It's not there!"

"What?" Emma raced down the hall and into the room, leaving him standing there watching her. It was true. Her forehead creased as she stepped closer to the sink and vanity, looking at the floor on each side to see if perhaps it had fallen. Nothing.

Her heart spiked along with the hair on the back of her neck. *It had been there earlier.* As far as she knew they'd all been together so no one had been in there to move it. Where the hell was it? The breath caught in her throat. Oh my God. Had Lily come in there while they were downstairs and got it? Was it now in the room with the two of them?

She shook her head at Frank and raced down the hall to pound on the door again. "Julia? What's going on? Did Lily take a hairbrush from the bathroom into the bedroom?" Her hands closed over her arms and she rubbed the skin briskly. It was so damned cold up there.

"Hang on!" The sounds of Julia's footsteps followed and her voice sounded on the other side of the door. "Lily's quieter now. She's just laying there like she's sleeping."

Emma's eyes closed as she exhaled a bit of tension. Julia was still scared but at least she wasn't terrified anymore. "A hairbrush, Julia! Is there an old hairbrush in the room?"

She felt rather than saw Frank close the gap between them and stand behind her.

"Why are you asking about an old hairbrush? *Just get us out of here!*" Julia was on the verge of tears. It was in her voice.

"*Just do it*! It's why we can't get the door open!" Emma didn't know how she knew this, but it had to be so. There was no logical explanation to any of this. "Lily took it from that creepy house! You need to find it."

The sounds of Julia's frantic footsteps and objects overturned and hitting the floor followed. Emma looked up at Frank. "What if it's in there? What do we do then?"

Frank straightened to his full six feet and his dark lips breathed out a long sigh. "It needs to go back where it was taken from. You disturbed the forces in that house. They won't rest until it's returned."

The door creaked, opening...slowly.

The sound and sight sliced through Emma's core making the hair on the back of her neck spike. Over at the bedroom window, Julia stood, her white nightgown shimmering in the moon's ray. Her dark eyes seemed to almost pop out onto cheeks that were pasty white, but it was her hand that sent a cold shiver up Emma's spine. Julia's fingers clutched the hairbrush.

A few feet away, Lily was flat on her back on the floor. A drool of pink spittle on her cheek was the only sign that she wasn't merely asleep, but rather unconscious from the ordeal.

Emma rushed forward, but stopped short when Frank gripped her arm spinning her around. "Stop! You can't touch her or the hairbrush! It's bad enough that it's here...that she has it in her hand." The whites of his eyes showed around ebony pupils and his mouth was a fierce gash.

"I'm going to—" Emma's words were cut short by the explosion of noise in the floor below her feet.

Blaring music interspersed with the cacophony of banging sounds, hard enough to shake the floor under her. She turned, her mouth wide with horror looking at her sister. Julia stood at the open window, tears rolling down her face, her shoulders wracking in sobs.

All hell had broken loose in the house and the cause of it was gripped in Julia's hand.

CHAPTER FIFTEEN

Julia's arm flew at the window opening. "I can't let go of it, Emma!" She reared back again, trying to throw the hairbrush through the opening. "*It won't let me let go of it!*" she shrieked. "It won't leggo!" Her face was terror stricken. "Help meeee!" Her knees fluttered. "I can't move my feet Emma!" She reached out to her sister, tears shining on her face.

Emma walked slowly over to her sister, standing outside her reach. Her heart broke seeing Julia standing helplessly crying. Why she couldn't touch her, take that blasted brush and throw it out the window, she didn't know. But in this, Frank knew what he was talking about. He knew.

Grace and Nana rushed into the bedroom, dropping down beside Lily.

Grandpa's eyes were blue chips of flint when he stepped up beside Frank and gripped his arm. "We've got to get that thing out of here! We need to end this, *tonight!*"

"Julia? We have to go back over to the Hanson house. We need to take the hair brush back. Don't worry. I'll be with you and once this is done, we'll be fine." It was hard to get around the lump in her throat, trying to keep her voice steady and calm. But she needed to be strong for Julia.

Julia looked down at her hand holding the brush, the silver

catching the light from the window behind her. All the while, the house was being ripped asunder by whatever was downstairs, the cacophony of noise ear splitting, shaking the floor under her feet.

Julia's lip quivered and more tears glistened in her eyes. "I can't move my feet! Even if I could, I won't go in there again." She began to hiccup.

Frank jostled Emma aside and squatted down in front of Julia. His voice even and deep, he looked into the eyes of the small girl. "You're a very brave Princess," he said. He held one hand out before her eyes, his other clutching something hanging around his neck. "You'll be brave now, hah?"

"I'm scared! Help meee!"

"Shhh... child," Frank said. "Now watch my hand and feel yourself grow still..." he began to move his hand from side to side. "Now just ignore all the noise and stormin' and watch my hand..." He repeated the phrase over and over again and Julia's eyes focused on his swaying hand. She began to rock slightly in time with his movement and her hiccupping eased.

"Now hold up the hairbrush brave one," Frank said, and Julia raised her hand. Frank focused his gaze upon the silver piece. "You! Listen! We'll return it! But you must let her step away now! We'll bring it back!" He kept his voice even, but Emma could hear in it a boiling rage and strength. "Release her."

Julia staggered, and looked down at her feet. She lifted one, then the other off the floor and looked at Frank in wonder.

"Now, Princess, be still and we'll be done soon." Frank stood up.

Emma stepped before her sister. "Grandpa and I will be right next to you." She ached to reach out and take Julia in her arms. Her sister was too fragile and small to have to do this. It wasn't her fault, any of this. She was innocent for God's sake!

"I'm coming too." Grace stood up and stepped next to Emma. "This is all my fault...and Lily's." Emma saw her cousin swipe a tear from her eye and look back at her sister. "She's going to be all right, isn't she Nana?" Her voice quivered.

Frank stepped to the door of the bedroom. "Come on! We'd better get this over with before the house blows apart!" He gestured with his hand and stepped to the side making room for them to leave. The cacophony downstairs had taken a breath and now resumed with higher fury.

"Go! Don't worry about Lily. I'll take care of her." Nana lifted Lily and held her in her arms, rocking back and forth. She looked up at Grandpa who was standing silently in the doorway. "Be careful, Dan."

He nodded and made his way down the hall, pausing at the newel post to look back at the rest of them. His stooped shoulders had never been lower. "I'll get the truck." With that he continued down the stairs and out of sight.

Emma fought back the tears when she gestured for Julia to come forward. She waited until Julia had passed her before moving. It was a horrible nightmare that she wished she could wake up from. But the maelstrom on the floor below was real!

"Just breathe, Julia. Try to think of something nice, like ice cream or swimming. We'll get through this." Emma was also trying to garner her own inner strength, stepping close behind Julia but not touching her.

"Or Mom and Dad?" Julia wailed, her shoulders heaving again. "I wanna go hoooome!"

Emma felt the final thread of her heart break following her sister. If only they had listened to their Grandpa. If only...She took a deep breath and squared her shoulders This wasn't helping. They had to just...get...through...this. Please God. All the while the floor below blared and shook, making her knees weak.

The three of them; Frank, Julia, then Emma with Grace at the back climbed down the stairs, holding the banister.

When they were halfway down, Grace piped up from the rear, "I'm so sorry, Julia! If I could take that from you, I would in a heartbeat. This is all my fault." Emma looked over her shoulder at her cousin. From the tears and tightness of her face, it was clear she meant it.

When they reached the kitchen doorway, Emma almost

walked right into Julia. Her sister had paused and shrank back at the sight there. Emma's heart nearly jumped from her chest and she froze staring into the room.

Every drawer of the kitchen cabinets opened quickly and then shut with a resounding bang! The doors on the cupboards swung wildly, back and forth before closing with a thundering clap! The elements of the stove glowed bright orange and the table rose and fell shuddering hard against the wooden floor. Nana's Mixmaster was floating a foot above the counter! The pots and frying pans were clanging where they hung from the rack! All the while the radio blasted and the sound of the television boomed from the living room.

Frank backed into the cabinets, holding the doors closed with his body and clearing a path through the mayhem. "HURRY!" His fist closed around the thing hanging from his neck again. He looked around the room and roared! "BY GOD, THAT'S ENOUGH!"

The mixer dropped like a stone, slamming to the counter. Emma's jaw fell open. The silence that followed Frank's words was palpable. Her ears rang from the suddenness of it. She could hear her heartbeat pound in her ears.

"Quick! Go! This won't last long." Frank gestured wildly with his arms for them to leave while his back strained hard against the cabinets. The vein in his forehead bulged and pulsed darkly.

The three girls scurried through the kitchen. When Emma passed Frank she looked up at him for a moment. What kind of power did the old man have that he could make it...*all the supernatural craziness* stop?

"GO!" His eyes protruded above a lined, leathery face.

She raced after her sister, through the kitchen and to the front door. Outside, at the end of the walkway, the truck sat idling, the headlights slicing the blackness of the night. Grandpa stood next to the tailgate, helping Grace up into the truck bed. He held up his hand when Julia approached. "Wait. Emma's next." He gestured to the front of the truck bed. "You two up there, right behind the cab." Turning to Julia, he said,

"You have to ride in the very back of the truck." His face softened. "I'm sorry, darlin', but it has to be that way. I wish it weren't, but it's bad enough business without endangering the others."

Emma climbed up into the truck and sat next to Grace. It was hard watching Julia roll into the back and cower at the edge. The tailgate clanged shut like the banging of a prison cell door.

Julia looked up and her eyes locked with Emma's. "I never told you how much I love you. Never said how proud I am to have you for a sister. If this doesn't work out, I thought you should know."

"Oh God..." Grace turned and looked away while it was all Emma could do not to scramble back to Julia and take her in her arms.

"Same goes for me, Jules. But in a little while all of this will be over. I'll be back to being the bossy older sister who grates your last nerve. You'll be the pain, you usually are." She swallowed the lump in her throat. "We'll get through this, okay?"

Julia nodded and the truck started down the road to the Hanson house. In the darkness that claimed them on the lonely road, Emma silently gave way to her tears.

Would they really get through this? Would anything ever be the same again?

CHAPTER SIXTEEN

The truck lurched to a halt at the iron gate, and its headlights illuminated the flagstone walkway leading to the house. Emma's breath stuck in her chest seeing the eerie light in the second floor window. This was it. They were here and there was no turning back. But that light was evidence that they wouldn't be alone. The house and whatever was in it, was waiting for them.

The thud of Grandpa's driver side door broke the stillness. He unhooked the tailgate and stepped back for Julia to get out.

Frank appeared on the other side of the truck. "I'll lead the way." His gaze took them all in and then settled on Julia. "No matter what happens, you stay focused on me. Follow me closely and don't stop. Got that?"

Julia nodded and she slipped off the truck, stepping closer to him. "But you don't know where Lily found it. How will you find the spot?" She was once more on the verge of tears, her shoulders low and sloped.

"I know where it was! I saw it on the dresser in the first bedroom when I was in there." Emma slid over the iron floor and lowered her feet to the ground. Her chin rose and she stared into his eyes. "I'm going with her. You can't stop me."

"Me too!" Grace hopped off the truck and clasped Emma's

hand in her own, giving it a quick squeeze. She turned to their grandfather. "I think you should stay at the door, to guard it and keep it open, Grandpa. We don't want to be in there any longer than we have to be and we need to be able to get out."

"She's got a point, Dan." Frank didn't give Grandpa a chance to argue; he turned and walked over to the gate. He shoved it open a foot or so, and then slipped through.

Emma couldn't help staring up at the glowing window as she followed behind Julia. It was the room where that horrid doll was...the room that had started all this when Grace saw it. Like the eye of the house, it watched their every move while luring them in.

Julia stumbled and cried out, catching herself before she landed on the dewy ground. Immediately, Frank swung the flashlight around, shining the light at her bare feet. "You all right?"

"No!" She adjusted the shoulder of her nightgown. "Do I look all right? Thanks to this..." holding the hairbrush high in the air, "...this stupid brush...I'm walking into a haunted house in the middle of the night! What's more...that stupid light up there isn't supposed to be on!" She shook her head and took a step forward. "*Am I all right?* Yeah. Next question, please." She threw her arms in the air. "*I want to kick that ghost in the face!*"

Emma couldn't help smiling. This was more like the feisty sister she knew and loved. If they were to get through this, she'd need a healthy dose of spunk. "Why don't you tell us how you really feel, Julia?" It was a line that their father used, teasing Julia when she was on a rant.

Julia turned, gazing into Emma's eyes. She nodded briskly and once more began to follow Frank. The boards of the step creaked in protest when Frank stepped up. He swung the light around for Julia to follow.

Emma took a step up, staying close to Julia. Every muscle in her body was tight and trembling. She stared ahead when Frank pushed the gaping door open further, the flashlight intruding into the dank darkness of the house. The stair railing and bottom step became visible and she shuddered, closing her eyes for a moment.

"Jesus, this is so creepy in here." Grace's words were barely above a whisper behind Emma.

"Don't take the Lord's name in vain, Grace. You may need His help to get through this." Grandpa stood like a sentry, his feet straddling the open doorway. "Just hurry and get this over with, okay? I'll be saying prayers down here."

Frank lowered the beam of the flashlight to light the steps and started up. When Emma followed, she folded her arms across her chest, rubbing her upper arms softly at the damp chill. Her gaze flitted through the inky air. It felt like there was someone or something watching them as they walked up the stairs.

A low creak broke the stillness...followed by a whispering shuffle...like footsteps! Emma froze. Julia gasped and turned, her hand reaching out to her sister.

"No!" Frank's head jerked around and their eyes met. When Julia pulled back, he turned and peered above to the top step.

"We come in peace." His voice echoed through the stairwell while his free hand clutched the amulet he wore around his neck. "We only want to return what belongs here."

The footsteps stopped but the air became even colder. If there were more light, she'd be able to see her breath in front of her face. There was no explanation for the sudden chill, anymore than there was for the footsteps that had sounded.

Frank's foot on the next stair creaked long and ominously. Emma took a deep breath. They were really going to do this. There was no turning back even though she wished that she was anywhere but there. Please God, if you're up there, help us! She took the next step and then the next, all the while chanting a prayer for God's help like a mantra in her mind.

Frank stood on the landing now, turning his light down to Julia's feet. It was working! They were almost there. It was so quiet that she could hear the others' breathing.

BANG! BANG! BANG!

The doors in all the bedrooms opened and slammed shut so hard that the house shook! Emma felt her heart hammer against her ribs. The noise was ear splitting while the house shook so hard, she scrabbled at the banister to stay on her feet. The light from the far bedroom pulsed with the door opening and shutting so fast. Frank and Julia were dark shadows while the air around them glowed in fast spurts.

The old man lurched to the side, shouldering the door of the first bedroom open and holding it. "Quick! Put it back!"

Julia turned and her eyes were wide and terrified peering at Emma. "I...I...can't....

"Yes you can! Do it quick before we're all killed!" Grace shouted and pushed forward to stand next to Emma.

Julia's eyes filled with tears and she started to slump down. Emma's teeth clenched. This was so unfair! She leapt forward and snatched the hairbrush from her sister without a second thought and darted into the room.

The vein in Frank's forehead was a dark line, every muscle in his body straining to keep the door from slamming shut. He had dropped the flashlight in order to grasp the door. It cast a faint beam across the floor.

As she looked around the room for the dresser she became aware of the cold numbness in her hand holding the brush. It was like a piece of ice, sending a cold ache up her arm. Oh my God! Julia had withstood all of that without a sound!

Seeing the dresser in the gloom, she stepped forward. There was a faint outline in the dust and she set it down in the exact place where it had lain for decades.

It was when she turned to leave that she saw the doll propped up on the bed. Its eyes blinked and then fell shut while it slumped over on the rumpled covers. Immediately silence descended in the house. All the doors that had been slamming shut stopped.

Emma watched the small plastic toy and felt her stomach roil. Just the sight of it there, laying on the bed made her skin crawl. It was the true evil in the house. Somehow, it was responsible for all of it. All the tragedy.

"Let's get out of here." Frank's voice broke into her thoughts and she jerked turning around. He reached for her and gripped her arm leading the way to the stairs.

She jerked back and stared up at him. "But that doll...We've got to destroy it. I just know it's evil...that it is somehow causing all this."

"We will! Hurry!" He grabbed her arm again and half carried her down the stairs. There was no way he was letting go of her. Her hand was numb, the one that had held the hairbrush and she held it close to her chest.

Downstairs, Julia, with Grace's arm over her shoulder walked by their grandfather as he stood in the doorway.

"Thank God, you're all right!" Grandpa reached out to her and took her in his arms, steering her onto the small front step. He kissed her forehead and then turned to Julia and Grace. "You girls go back to the truck! Frank and I will finish this."

"Wait!" Frank stepped forward and handed her something in his palm. "Take this. Hold it tight in your hand. It'll help."

Emma looked down at the small stone and the loop of leather draped through a hole in the dead centre. She closed her fingers over it, pressing it into her palm. At first it was just a slight tingle and then it began to get warmer. She looked up at him. "Thanks."

"Now go. Get over to the truck and stay there." Frank turned to her grandpa and the look on his face was grim. "We know what we have to do."

Grandpa ran his hand through his hair. "We should have done it years ago, Frank."

"Ayuh... well, better late than never..." Frank's face split in the first smile Emma had ever seen, "Kemosabi!" The two men chuckled.

Emma's gaze flickered between each of the men before she turned and walked after her sister and cousin. She felt like she was in a dream, a very bad dream. But the ache in her hand was real.

She slipped through the gate and joined Julia, pulling her into her arms and stroking her hair. "We're safe. It's over now."

"Not quite." Grace's cheekbones were highlighted with streaks of gold and her eyes shone as she stared at the Hanson house.

Emma turned and saw the licks of flame, rising from the front door and the broken front window. The two men were dark silhouettes moving in the orange light.

"Thank God. No one will ever go in there again. And that evil doll will be destroyed." Emma smiled and pulled her sister tighter into her body.

CHAPTER SEVENTEEN

With all that had gone on, they were back home less than an hour after leaving. They left Hanson House to burn on its own; Grandpa didn't want to hang around to answer any questions from the firemen or police.

Upon entering, the first thing that Emma noticed was the quiet. Everything was as it should be—no doors banging, no table crashing against the floor or things flying through the air. She'd never appreciated how good normal could be.

Nana got up from the kitchen table where she'd been sitting next to Lily. There were tears in her eyes when she rushed over and folded the three girls into her arms. "Thank God!"

Emma felt like she'd run a marathon race. Every muscle in her body was heavy and warm. Even her hand had returned to normal, although she still clutched the stone amulet tightly. Hopefully, Frank wouldn't ask for it back. There was a sense of power and calm that holding it brought—obviously why he always wore it. Her head tilted to the side. Maybe that was why her aunt wore hers.

Grace slipped out of her Nana's arms and went over to the table to sit next to Lily. "Are you okay now?" She put her arm over the thin child's shoulders and hugged her, giving her a kiss on the cheek. "You had me worried!" When she drew back, tears glistened in her eyes.

"Come in! Have some hot chocolate. I'd say have some tea but I think you'd rather have chocolate. It fixes everything." Nana led Emma and Julia over to the table. She turned and her hand rested on Grandpa's arm. "Thank God. It's finally over now, isn't it?"

He nodded and then pulled out the chair at the head of the table to take a seat. "Frank? Stay and have some tea...or maybe a shot of whiskey might be more in order."

Frank smiled. "I'll take you up on the whiskey, but I've got something to do first. I'll be right back."

Emma stared wide eyed and smiling at the older man walking across the floor to go out the back door. He'd got them through this. Just like he'd helped her grandfather so many years ago. And his smile had been nice. It was the first time she'd actually seen it.

"What was it like over there?" Lily hunched over the cup of hot chocolate that she'd been drinking, peering closely at Emma and Grace.

"It was a real walk in the park! What did you think it'd be like? No thanks to you!" Julia scowled and then looked down at her hand, holding her wrist, and flexing her fingers. Her face softened when she looked over at Lily. The poor kid was close to tears.

"I'm sorry. I don't know why I took it...the hairbrush. It was kind of like a voice in my head telling me to take it." Lily looked down into the dark brown liquid, cupping her hands around the mug.

"Yeah right! We could have—"

"Julia! Stop. I think she's telling the truth. There was something in that house that was really bad. Right from the start it spoke to her. Don't blame Lily." A flash of the doll, its eyes sliding shut and then it falling to the side flashed in Emma's mind and she shuddered.

She turned to her grandfather. "The fire...will the fire department be able to stop it?" That was the last thing she wanted. The house was evil. How many people had to die or get hurt before it was destroyed?

Her grandfather's eyebrows rose and he shrugged. "It was going pretty good when we left. All that dry wood. It'd be a miracle if they did. It's mostly volunteers so who knows when they'd get there." He sighed and looked up at Nana who was stirring milk into a saucepan on the stove. "It's high time someone destroyed it."

When the back door banged shut, Emma jerked in her seat, but calmed when she saw it was Frank. The night had been way too creepy for any sudden noises. She stifled a yawn. She was beat to a snot, but knew it would be hours before she'd be able to fall asleep.

Frank sat down at the table. He set three stone amulets in front of him. Each of them had a hole where a loop of leather threaded through, forming a necklace. "These are for you girls." His eyes met Emma's. "How's your hand?"

"Better. I don't know why but I think this helped." She held the amulet up by its string.

"Good." He picked up a small black one and handed it to Julia. "Take this. It'll help." He slid the other two across the table in front of Grace and Lily. "They're not the prettiest things in the world but they'll give you some protection against bad spirits. You encountered more than a few today."

Lily picked hers up and looped it over her neck. She looked up at him and smiled. "It's like the one Mom wears."

"Where do you think she got it? Your mother paid a visit to the Hanson house when she was your age. She was lucky I spotted her heading that way and got her out of there." Frank sat back when Grandpa put a glass of amber liquid in front of him. He looked up at Grandpa and grinned. "You never knew that. I knew you'd have a conniption if you did. It was our secret, Cynthia and me."

Grace slipped her necklace over her head and held the amulet up, examining it with her eyes. "It's pretty, in a primitive sort of way." She smiled at Frank. "Thank you. And thanks for everything you did today. I can't imagine what would have happened if you didn't check on us." She shuddered.

Emma looked over at Grace. Was this the same girl who'd been so snotty about Frank when they'd got there? "So it really is the end of that house, isn't it?" It was hard to believe how much they'd gone through and that they'd got out relatively unscathed.

Lily leaned forward peering at Grandpa. "Does this mean, we can stay?" Some colour had returned to her cheeks and her eyes were bright.

He smiled and set his glass of whiskey down on the table. "We'll see how you are in the morning. Although you look fine now, we can't be too careful. It was scary seeing you like that earlier." I want to make sure you're really okay."

Nana rested her hand on Lily's shoulder and looked down at her. "You were out cold for about fifteen minutes you know. You scared the life out of me. You're sure you feel okay now?"

Lily looked up at her. "Just a little headache and I'm really tired. But other than that, I'm okay."

Frank polished off the whiskey in one fell swoop and then sighed. "Well, that's it for me. I'm off to bed." He got to his feet slowly and looked at each of the girls in turn. "It was a foolish thing you did earlier today, but I'd be lying if I didn't say, it's no surprise. Your Grandpa and me did something like that when we were your age." He turned to Grace. "As did your mother. But it's over now." He glanced out the kitchen window. "And it'll never happen again."

Grandpa stood up and he clasped Frank's hand in both of his. "Take your time getting up in the morning. The chores will still be there at noon and the animals won't starve." He held Frank's hand for an extra few seconds and looked in his eyes. "We owe you a lot, Frank. Thanks."

Cracking another rare smile, Frank said, "It's a full time job keeping an eye on your family." Nodding, he turned left. Nana's head fell to the side, "And you kids should go to bed too. Finish your hot chocolate and try to get some sleep."

Emma nodded to Julia and they rose, placing the empty mugs in the sink. When she turned Grace and Lily were following suit. Probably Grandpa and Nana needed some time to decompress and talk.

When they got upstairs, they couldn't help standing at the window to watch the inferno that now flared across the field. The glow of bright yellow and orange flames pierced the dark night sky. Headlights of a few vehicles raced towards the building but Emma knew they had arrived too late, which was just as well.

It was all over for the Hanson house.

CHAPTER EIGHTEEN

Rays of sunshine beamed into the window, infusing the bedroom with a warm golden glow when Emma opened her eyes. As she was about to stretch the sleep from her muscles, she noticed Julia beside her, curled up next to the wall, still sleeping soundly. The innocence of her sister's face was angelic. It was hard to reconcile what had happened yesterday with the peaceful child sleeping beside her. The night over at the Hanson house had been like a bad dream.

She slipped out from under the coverlet being careful not to disturb Julia. As she was passing the other set of bunk beds on her way out of the room, Grace's eyes popped open. "Wait up. Let's check the window—see if it's really gone."

Grace's bare feet slid onto the floor and she rose, scampering quickly over to check it out. When Emma joined her there she gave a sigh of relief. For some reason, she hadn't expected it to be gone. But tendrils of smoke drifting up from the blackened heap were all that was left of the horrible house.

"I'm glad I have the photos." Grace nudged Emma with her shoulder. "Don't worry. I'm leaving the memory stick in the barn until we leave. There's no way I'm going to tempt fate...not after what happened last night."

Emma smiled. "Thanks." She nodded her head gesturing

for them to leave the room and let the others sleep. When they were in the hall, she turned to catch Grace before she disappeared into the bathroom. "I hope you write a great story. You'll send it to me won't you?"

When Grace paused and looked over at her, Emma noticed the stone amulet hanging around Grace's neck. Somehow, seeing her wear it made Grace seem more vulnerable. The fashionista from New York City was perfectly willing to wear the primitive stone that Frank had fashioned. Her fingers went up to hold her own amulet.

"Absolutely. You and Julia might even make it to the dedication page." She grinned and went into the bathroom.

Emma turned and continued down the stairs to join her grandparents at breakfast. When she entered the room they looked up from their places at the old kitchen table. Everything was back to normal even if they'd all gotten a later start to the day.

"I just got off the phone with your Dad. He wanted to know how you and Julia are making out with your cousins." Grandpa chuckled seeing the look of silent curiosity in her eyes. "I didn't tell him about the Hanson house or anything. There was no sense in worrying him. It's all over now."

Emma's breathed a short sigh. That meant that they were going to finish the vacation with their grandparents. They wouldn't be sent home and their father would never know. Not unless... "Did you know that Grace is planning on writing a book about the Hanson house?"

Nana's head drew back and her eyebrows rose high. "Is she? I never knew she wanted to be a writer." She rose to her feet. "What would you like for breakfast? There's pancakes warm in the oven."

Emma kissed her grandmother's velvety, lined cheek when she passed her. "That'd be lovely, Nan." Her chest swelled with love for her grandparents. The morning was a new beginning to the vacation, the horror had passed. As she took a seat beside her grandpa she smiled. "After we finish the chores today, I'd like to go swimming at the beach. For real this time."

Grandpa chuckled. "I'm not worried. There's nothing over at that place to tempt you anymore, not unless the prospect of getting full of soot appeals to you." He picked up his mug of coffee and took a long sip.

"Where's Frank? Has he already finished breakfast?" Emma was surprised to find that she kind of missed seeing him at the table.

"You just missed him too, I'm afraid. He's probably feeding the pigs by now." Nana set the plate of pancakes in front of Emma. "We all slept in but I think we deserved it."

Grace entered the kitchen, tugging the belt on her sky blue robe tight around her waist. "Good morning!" The pony tail she'd swept her hair up into swayed as she sauntered over to the stove. When Nana made a move to join her there, she held her hand up. "No. I'll get this. You sit down and relax, Nana. You wait on us too much."

Emma's eyes opened wider. For Grace to do this was unusual. She was always so regal expecting everyone to attend to her needs. Even her hair was a little unkempt with straggles falling over her high cheekbones. Grace piled a few pancakes on a plate and then pulled out a chair to join them.

At the thud of footsteps coming down the stairs, everyone turned to see Lily and Julia saunter into the room. If Lily was suffering any after effects from the night before she sure wasn't showing it. In fact, her cheeks were rosy and her eyes sparkled, clear as a bell. Julia was her usual mess of curls and giggles as she skipped over to the table and planted a kiss on grandpa's cheek.

Lily poured a glass of milk and smiled over at them. "What's up for today? Anymore haunted houses on the island for us to visit?" She laughed as she walked over to the table, her head high and no longer slouching.

"Once is plenty for me!" Grace said with a wave of her hand. She pulled out a chair for her sister to sit next to her. "I thought we'd do something conventional like maybe weeding the garden. That's enough excitement for today, I think."

Emma had never seen the two of them so easy with each

other, let alone the rest of the family. Last night really affected them, but in this manner was a surprise. She'd never seen Grace actually cry over anyone or anything, but she had last night.

"Well that's good to hear. The garden is a mess. The weeds are choking out the vegetables." Nana looked over at Julia. "How about you? How are you feeling?"

"I'm fine now. My hand still tingles a little but it's better. I think I'm sworn off scary movies. I don't know how you could even think about going to any other haunted house, Lily." She went to the stove and took the plate of pancakes from the oven.

"I was just kidding, silly! When I saw that house all black and still smoking, it made me happy. I'm glad it's gone." Lily smiled and bit into her breakfast.

"It's going to be a scorcher today. I think you girls should leave the weeding till tomorrow. Go to the beach and relax." Grandpa rose to his feet. "I'm going to help Frank finish up outside. I'm sure he'd like to take it easier today as well...especially after last night."

Emma leaned over the table looking up at her grandfather. "Will you get into trouble for starting that fire over there? Will anyone investigate it?" She'd seen a lot of crime stories and this was something she'd wondered about last night. But last night, had definitely not been the time to bring it up. Not when everything was so fresh and scary.

He paused and the smile left his face. "As far as anyone on the island is concerned it was a blessing to see it destroyed. As for us...no one ever need know about it." He smiled at Grace. "I hear you're writing a fiction book."

Her eyes went wide and she sat straighter in her chair. "Yes. Only fiction. No real names or places."

"Good. Now I'm off to help Frank." With that Grandpa left the room.

***

It was almost two by the time the girls rolled their bicycles off the path at the beach. The morning had gone smoothly with all of them pitching in to clean up and help with lunch— even Grace. When Emma looked over at her cousin, she couldn't help wondering if this was the same girl who'd irritated the heck out of her when she arrived. Grace couldn't have been nicer that morning.

Lily set her bicycle down on the grass and turned to look over at the Hanson ruins. Tendrils of smoke still drifted aimlessly in the still air from the burned out hulk. "I don't feel anything about that house now. Isn't that strange? It's as if whatever was there left with the fire. No voices in my head, nothing."

Grace set her bike down and walked over to her sister. She looped her arm over the thin girl's shoulders and gazed up at the old burnt out husk. "If I had any idea that going over there would have affected you like that, I would have burnt it myself. Thank God Grandpa did."

Emma let her bike slip to the ground and then followed Julia down to the shoreline. The water was a clear blue slate with hardly a ripple to mar its surface. She gazed up at the sky, shielding her eyes from the bright glare of the afternoon sun.

"What's that?" Julia pointed to an object bobbing in the water about twenty feet out.

Emma squinted her eyes peering to where her sister indicated. Sure enough, there was something floating in the water...something about the size of a loaf of bread, bobbing gently. She could barely make it out but there was a flash of pale pink. When she leaned over, peering hard, her mouth fell open. It seemed like a small face, the roundness above topped with a dark shadow.

She jumped when Lily stepped close to her. "Oh no. It can't be..." Lilly's voice was flat.

Emma spun to face her, saw the same blank look on her face as she'd worn the day before, going into the Hanson house. Emma turned back to the object and waded farther out into the water, never letting it out of her sight. When she was a couple feet from it, she gasped.

It was the doll from the Hanson house. The only difference in it now was that the hair was gone, replaced by charred soot, the plastic melted to the scalp. One if its eyes stared sightlessly at her. A shiver crept through her shoulders as she stood frozen in place.

This couldn't be! The doll had been in that room! It should have burned up with the rest of it!

Her hand rose to clasp the amulet hanging over her chest. She turned, and started back up to the beach where Julia and her cousins stood. Her eyes met with Grace's. "It's that doll! That thing that was in the Hanson house! Hurry, let's get out of here!"

Grace's hand clasped her arm on the way by, stopping her. "Wait!" Her eyes were wide and she looked as scared as Emma felt. Already Julia was at the edge of the beach, picking her bike up from the ground.

"Why? I know it's the one! It shouldn't be here! It's like it knew we were coming here today...waiting to scare the life out of us again." Emma turned back and scowled at the doll that bobbed nonchalantly in the gentle surf. That bloody thing! Would this ever be over?

"We need to take it back there." Grace raised her hands high in exasperation. "Don't you see? It's not over! This is a sign."

"Are you nuts? I'm not going back to that place...no way!" Emma continued on her way, the smooth rounded beach rocks shifting under her strides.

Lily raced after her and gripped her shoulder. "Wait. She's right. We need to take care of this. The doll needs to be destroyed. But not there! Not back at that horrible place." Her fingers clasped the amulet that hung around her neck. "We'll sink it."

Emma shook her head. "That won't work. If the fire didn't destroy it, the thing is indestructible. We need to get Frank and Grandpa." But how on earth had it moved? The fire had been a blaze when they'd left the Hanson house. No one could have been in there to survive and get the doll out. She glanced out at the object and shuddered seeing it come closer to the shore. Pushed by whatever current was there. A thought flashed in her mind that made her knees weak. *It's coming for them.*

"No. This will work. I know it." Again, Lily had that far away look in her eyes.

Emma gaped at her cousin wild eyed. "Are you crazy?"

"No," Lily said. "I know this to be true." Just like yesterday, her voice had flattened.

But when she glanced at Emma, there was another aspect to her expression. Her lips were set in a determined line, not slack like they were the day before. She'd been the one who had heard the voices, sensed the presence of spirits in that house. Maybe she was right about this.

Grace stepped over and put her hand on Lily's shoulder. "I believe you. We've got to do this, don't we?"

Lily nodded. "Grandpa and Frank finished the house. It's up to us to finish this part." She looked over at Emma. "You were right yesterday, you know. You knew that the doll was evil. It *is*. We have to destroy it."

Julia set her bike down and joined the other three. "You can't do it here at our beach. I'll never go swimming here again knowing that thing's at the bottom." Her lips were pursed as she scowled out at the floating doll. "That thing just ruins everything for us."

"You're right. We'll take it farther down the beach, to the Hanson's property. Then we sink it. Maybe water will do what fire couldn't." Grace turned and stared at the doll. It was only about twelve feet away by now.

"Right! How are we going to do that? I'm not touching it!" Julia stepped closer to Emma and nudged her. "C'mon. Let's go and get Grandpa or Frank." She started back towards her bike.

Grace called after her. "Wait! I think we all need to stick together to finish this. We can poke it with a stick. None of us has to touch it."

"Come back, Julia. We can do this. Actually it has to be us,

I think. It was a child's toy...so we have to do it." Lily started walking up the beach towards the Hanson waterfront.

Emma stood looking at the doll, trying to digest Lily's words. The young girl seemed so sure of all of this. Even Grace was on side, willing to take care of it and not upset her grandparents any further. God only knows, they'd been through enough with all of this.

"But how are we going to sink it, if we don't touch the thing?" She turned and started following Lily and Grace. "C'mon Julia. Just this last time. I think she's right. Maybe the water will destroy its power".

Grace picked up a long branch that had washed up on the shore. "We'll tie a big rock to it. We've got the laces in our sneakers and God knows there's no shortage of rocks on this beach." She waded into the water and then held the stick next to the doll, pushing it farther along.

Again, Julia set her bike down and rushed to catch up with Emma. They watched Grace slip on a slimy rock and catch herself just before she toppled in. The doll had gone under but popped up again, the eyes open and blank. Even though she had no wish to go any closer to that doll, Emma could see that Grace needed help. The rocks submerged at the beach were slippery and coated in satiny seaweed. Besides her sneakers were already wet.

She waded in and reached for Grace's free hand. "Here. Hold my hand. We'll keep each other from falling in."

Grace smiled. "Thanks. I'm glad you and Julia decided to stay and help with this." Her smile fell. "This is my fault and I have to see it through."

"No, I don't think this is all your fault, Grace." Emma looked over at the shoreline where Julia and Lily walked side by side. She turned to Grace and smiled. "We all have to do this...it's not just your fault. You didn't twist anyone's arm. The four of us got into this together, and that's how we're going to finish it."

They walked a few more steps seeing Lily and Julia up ahead, stopped at the beach that was part of the Hanson property. Grace sighed and gave the doll the last big push. They stood watching as it rolled onto its belly with only the flimsy dress floating above it.

Grace turned to her before continuing on. She squeezed Emma's hand and there were tears in her eyes when she spoke. "You know? If I had to be stuck here for a month on this farm, I'm glad you and Julia were here too."

Emma felt her chest expand and she squeezed Grace's hand right back. "What would you expect? We're cousins. We can do this."

Emma turned and waded through the water going up to the short shoreline of the Hanson farm. Lily and Julia were already crouched low, threading the laces from their sneakers. She glanced over to the water and the hair on the back of her neck spiked seeing the small ancient doll bobbing in the water. Grace gave it one final poke and then joined them on the shore.

Taking a heavy square shaped rock in her hand Emma looped her laces over it, making it look like some garish boxed gift. She took the laces that Lily and Julia had and tied the ends to hers, making a long rope of them. She watched Grace form a noose with hers and then take the lace end from her hand.

She hefted the rock up and shadowed Grace back into the water. Behind her she could hear the ripples that Lily and Julia's feet made, following them. Taking care not to actually touch the doll, Grace spread the loop and tugged it so that it slipped over the doll's head. She gave another yank and it tightened around the neck.

"Should we say some sort of prayer before I throw this rock out there?" Emma looked over at Lily who seemed to be the one most in tune with this kind of thing.

Lily gazed at the doll and sighed. "Just throw it. The sooner it lays on the bottom of the lake, the better. It doesn't deserve any prayers or any more of our attention. Let's just get rid of it."

Julia snickered. "Amen!"

Emma hoisted the rock and threw it for all she was worth.

The doll went air borne for a couple of seconds before being swallowed in the loud splash of the heavy rock. She felt Julia's hand close over hers and then turned when Grace took her other hand. The four girls stood in a line knee deep in the lake, united by their hands and hearts.

It marked the start of the last summer vacation on their grandparent's farm. A summer where they left the rivalries and petty grievances of young girls. To not only become women, but close friends who'd been tried and tested by an evil, haunting experience. Much like their grandfather and Frank had so many years ago.

The End

AUTHOR'S NOTE

Kingston, Ontario lies along an area known as the Thousand Islands region. The sizes of these islands range from tiny to large as a small city. Surrounded on all sides by water, they hold their own mysteries and secrets.

The sometimes cryptic nature of the Thousand Islands served as the jumping off point for this tale of The Hauntings of Kingston. Yes, bootlegging, or rum-running as it was also known in these parts, played a significant role in the economy of this area during the 1920's. The book Booze, Boats and Billions by C.W. Hunt is a fascinating read about the area's history during this era.

Thank you for reading The Ghosts of Hanson House. I hope you enjoyed this tale as much as I enjoyed writing it. If you could leave an honest review on Amazon I would greatly appreciate it. Reviews are ambrosia to new authors as they try to establish a career, but more importantly, your honest opinion will help other readers such as yourself make informed decisions on how to spend their precious time.

ABOUT THE AUTHOR

A lifelong resident of Kingston, Michelle has experienced firsthand, eerie events. She's witnessed episodes where the veil between our world and the next has shimmered gossamer thin. These encounters fascinate rather than frighten her. On the other hand, her two pugs Ruby and Sookie freak out enough for the three of them. The Irish part of her heritage, stories of banshees, druids and, yes, leprechauns are what started her down the road of writing about the paranormal.

In the summer she dreams about skiing, and in the winter wishes she lived in Cuba. Yes, she's contrary as hell, but never boring. She hopes you enjoy reading her work as much as she enjoys writing it. She is currently practicing her acceptance speech for the Nobel Prize in Literature just in case. LOL

Michelle is on Facebook, just like half the planet, or you can reach out to her via her Author page on Amazon.com.

Made in the USA
Monee, IL
15 January 2021

57752712R00075